THE HARLOT'S HORDE

by

NIKKI DEE

Being book three of the Sansome Springs Saga

Copyright © 2019 Nikki Dee

ISBN: 978-1792818738

In memory of

David 'Dave' Klages June 2017

and

Eileen 'Pean' Smith July 2017

Nikki Dee

The Harlot's Garden
The Harlot's Pride
The Harlot's Horde
Losing Hope
An Ordinary Girl

www.nikkidee.net

PROLOGUE 1810

The boy groaned and shifted in a bid to escape the hand that shook him. Even in his half-conscious state he knew there was a world of pain waiting for him and he'd delay it if he could.

He sensed, rather than saw, the kick that was aimed at him and rolled over in time to dodge it. His stomach churned with the movement and he vomited copiously, wincing as he re-tasted the stolen brandy he'd guzzled the night before.

Memories came in bursts. Fleeting, but enough to explain why he felt as deathly as he did. The challenge - one he'd thrown out - was to smuggle as many stolen bottles of wine as possible to the out-of-bounds tower room. Those who brought the greatest haul decided who could stay and join in the drunken revelry.

The games had been his idea and he rather thought he'd drunk most of what was on offer.

Dammit, Pa would give him hell if he was found out, he was on a last warning as it was.

'Wake up you idiot.' A voice said, just a second before a basin of cold water was dashed into his face.

He spluttered and gasped for breath. 'Christ, did you have to? Is it Pa?'

'It's more serious than that, get up and look out of the window.'

'What the hell's wrong with you?'

'Come and see for yourself.'

He put his feet on the ground and shook his head. The room swayed back and forth and gripped a corner beam and clung on with one hand as he wiped away the water dripping from his hair with the other.

It took all his concentration to navigate the uneven wooden floorboards, but he reached the window in one piece, and without vomiting again. He leaned heavily against the window sill and shot an irritated look at his friend. If this was his idea of a bloody joke…

Several of the school masters were gathered together in a busy knot in the square two floors below, their voices raised in disagreement. Interesting, the masters always presented a united face in public. He couldn't make out their words, but the frantic arm waving and nervous pacing told him something momentous was being played out. His curiosity kept him upright and attentive.

It looked for all the world as though Johnson, the nervous Latin master, was facing up to Baxter, an absolute beast on the rugger field and a bully off it. This should be quite a show.

He leaned further out, unwilling to miss anything and that's when he saw the still and broken body of a small boy lying at the base of the tower, perfectly peaceful, though surrounded by chaos.

He blinked rapidly and looked again, only to see a woman run through the gates toward the group of men, her desperate voice carrying up to him. 'What's happened to my boy? What have you done to him?'

One of the masters moved forward and clasped her tightly, preventing her from touching the small body. She fought to get away, punching the man's chest and wailing out her grief.

'Tommy Chambers. Fell off the tower.'

'Oh God. When? How?'

His friend shrugged and the pity in his eyes was plain to see. 'You were just fooling around, I know that. I'll stand by you, but we must get our story straight and stick to it. We shouldn't have been up here - so we weren't! If anyone asks, we were in our room all night and we heard and saw nothing.'

He swallowed deeply, frantically trying to bring the events of the night into his mind. Drinking and challenging one another, there'd been plenty of pushing and shoving, but nothing... 'We can't lie.'

His friend shook him until his teeth rattled. 'We can't risk ruining your future for a prank that went wrong. I doubt the family business could withstand such a scandal and it wasn't your fault anyway.'

He watched numbly as his friend bent to pick up an empty bottle, discarded the previous night. 'Move yourself! We'll clean up in here and get back downstairs while everyone's busy. Friends stick together no matter what. Agreed?'

He nodded, wishing he could remember last night. He'd done something terrible, but why couldn't he bring it to mind? He bent to gather up empty bottles and jugs.

The balance of power shifted.

CHAPTER ONE 1820

MARY

The thing with Ruby Morgan is she's pig-headed. If she makes up her mind to do a thing, then it will be done. No matter how wrong headed an idea is, she won't back down for fear of showing weakness. She can't abide weakness.

She'd planned to take Emily with her to Sansome Springs and she was not about to change her mind, whatever the weather.

She and Eliza, who is fast learning how to be as pig headed, agreed months back the twins, Emily and Georgie, were too wrapped up in each other and needed to be eased apart.

They decided that every Thursday they'd each take a twin and involve them in separate activities. The twins fought the idea, like they fought everything anybody else suggested, but like I say, she's pig headed.

Ruby needed to spend a couple of hours with the manager out at the pleasure gardens, and she was fixed on taking Emily with her, leaving Eliza at home and continuing to get Georgie interested in the accounts. A fool's errand if ever I heard of one.

A storm was promised for later, but Ruby was confident she could get to Sansome Springs and back ahead of it, and if those bloody twins hadn't played up she would have.

They knew her plans, but still the silly little madams came down stairs together wearing white dresses with satin slippers, as though they were going to a fancy tea or a ball. Their thinking was she'd be impatient to get off and would go without Emily, sooner than wait for her to change.

Not Ruby! She sent Emily back up to get changed and that delayed them by an hour, but off they went, Emily as miserable as sin and Ruby stubborn as a mule.

Eliza took Georgie into the parlour with the account books, and I tucked myself up nice and warm in the kitchen with Juliet, both of us thankful to be in the dry. We could always find plenty to talk about.

Juliet was forever mithering her future, she'd been taken on as a companion to the girls when they first came to us, nigh on babies they'd been then. Now they're almost grown up and she don't have a fat lot to be honest. If it'd been me, I'd have put me feet up and kept me head down, but Juliet's a stickler for doing the right thing.

They'd been gone two hours when the storm hit us, and by Christ it hit hard. I've never seen or heard the like. It felled the tree that had stood outside since I was girl. I heard windows breaking upstairs and I watched the old chimney fall into the yard.

I thought about Ruby, out in it and I knew... I don't know what I knew, but it was bad.

Eliza and Georgie came scurrying into the kitchen to wait with us. I could see they were scared to death, poor little buggers, but I had no comfort for them. Holding my own fright close was all I could manage.

We couldn't hear ourselves talk above the howling of the wind, not that we had anything to say by then.

We sat there together through the night, all four of us, waiting, and praying.

CHAPTER TWO

The sound of hammering echoed through the house and Eliza jerked upright, wincing at the stiffness in her back. The room was cold, the fire dead, she must have slept for a couple of hours.

She heard the others following her down the hallway, but she couldn't look their way. She so badly wanted to see Ruby and Emily there that she was almost afraid to open the door.

As she slid back the bolt the heavy door was whipped out of her hands and thrown against the wall, cracking the mirror that hung there for as long as she could remember, and letting in a gust of icy wind.

Mary muttered about bad luck, but Eliza ignored her as she waved the two waiting men inside. Her stomach churned, her heart was in her mouth and she tried to hold herself together even as she sensed the news she was about to hear.

She was unable to speak, but Georgie, red faced and with swollen eyes, begged them to tell them what they knew. 'Please don't make us wait.'

The shorter of the two men nodded to Eliza, even as he walked towards the fire. 'Won't you sit, Miss?'

She shook her head.

'Well, we have bad news for you. We've found the body of Mrs Morgan and young Emily, well, she's been taken to the infirmary. They were found together, out by the springs.'

He swallowed and whipped off his hat, tipping a nod to the other man, who quickly did the same.

Mary moaned once and slipped into a chair, head bowed and shoulders shaking.

Eliza opened her mouth, sucked in air and clapped a hand to her stomach. 'The body? Ruby was dead, but that was inconceivable, there had to be a mistake. She closed her eyes and muttered a prayer.

'I'm awful sorry miss.'

She opened her eyes, and they were all standing in a half circle around her, watching her face and waiting for her to tell them what to do.

Fear flooded through her, she wanted to cry, to scream her refusal to be fooled by their wicked lies. Pain twisted in her chest and she gasped for breath, barely able to remain upright.

Georgie howled, Mary sobbed, and Juliet stood helpless, rooted to the spot. Ruby really was dead.

Georgie threw herself into Eliza's arms and they clung on to each other.

'Our sister, Emily?' Eliza asked. 'What more can you tell us?'

It appeared that Emily had been pinned to the ground by Ruby's body. The iron bar that had killed Ruby lay across the two of them, the most likely explanation was that Ruby had thrown herself across Emily to save her life.

There was no way of knowing whether Ruby had been killed straight away, or at what time the accident occurred as Emily was in an unresponsive state.

'We had the young lady taken to the infirmary because she was alive, but not awake, if you understand me. We couldn't know how hurt she was. You'll have to go there and see to her.'

'But she'll recover? Is that what you're saying?'

He shrugged, not unkindly. 'You'll need to talk to the doctor at the infirmary about that, but she didn't look to good to me.'

A cold loneliness washed in and settled down inside her. What was she supposed to do first, how was she to manage on her own? She felt sick and her vision blurred, she leaned against the wall before she fell.

It was too much, she wasn't going to be able to cope, it was as simple as that. She closed her eyes and felt her knees soften. *Oh, Ruby, tell me what to do?*

Georgie's frightened scream brought her to her senses. 'We have to go to the infirmary now. Emily needs us.'

Eliza nodded. She reached into the cupboard and pulled out two heavy cloaks. 'Get dressed and we'll go and find her. Don't cry now, we'll bring her home.'

As Georgie bent to change into sturdy shoes Eliza quickly wrapped her arms around the unbending body of Mary and looked up at Juliet. 'I'll be home as soon as I can.'

Juliet nodded and clasped Eliza's hand. Her face pale, but brave. 'Don't worry about anything but Emily. I'll see to Mary.'

CHAPTER THREE

The scene they stepped out into was one of shocking contrast. The sky was a brilliant, bright blue, and the air was icy and fresh, but the ground they walked on was unrecognisable.

The track that they had walked on all their lives had gone, landmarks they'd always know were washed away, and everything was coated in a sea of slime and mud, a sea that was strewn with such an array of debris Eliza struggled to take it all in.

She shuddered as she realised the shape that had crushed part of their hedge was a dead sheep. The little house next door had been reduced to a pile of rubble, topped with the half-buried carcass of a cow. The heavier branches of their own oak tree lay smashed through the remains of the stables.

She pictured the soft velvety nose of Ned and she could almost smell him, the warm and gentle keeper of her secrets. She stifled a sob and pinched herself hard to stop it.

Her beloved Ruby was dead, her sister badly injured, how on earth could she possibly cry about a dead horse?

She reached for Georgie's hand and they walked on in stunned silence. Not a house along the length of The Foregate was undamaged. They saw shattered windows, doors hanging drunkenly and fences that had been torn up and now perched dangerously across the roof tops they'd landed on.

People stood about, friends and neighbours, surveying the horror. Shocked, drawn faces attempting to come to terms with their own loss and barely able to console others.

An angry shout rang out, followed by another, alerting them to see a gang of strangers, climbing over the rubble, picking through the damage and trying to salvage what they could use. Scuffles broke out as the exhausted home owners desperately fought to protect what was left of their property, but they were no match for the thieves and were picked off with ease.

One old man waved his stick furiously. 'You bastard rats, robbing them as has nothing left, may you rot in hell.' A gob of phlegm sent to accompany the words aroused only jeers and laughter from the gang.

'Eliza, I'm scared.' Georgie whimpered.

Eliza shivered, feeling the menace that swirled around them but refusing to be cowed. 'Do not start crying.' She said firmly. 'Take my arm, keep your eyes on the ground, and walk.'

They linked arms and slipped and skidded through the mud. By the time they reached the infirmary they were both cold, tired and coated with mud, but their fears for Emily overrode discomfort.

The infirmary was surrounded by a shouting mob as people in all manner of distress clamoured to get through the doors.

Eliza paused to catch her breath and prepared for a fight. She held a picture of sweet Emily in her head and forced her way through, pushing past people with gashed faces or oddly twisted limbs – losing contact with Georgie in the melee - and ignoring the complaints and shaking off the hands that tried to pull her back.

'I see you pushing yourself to the front, you little bitch. Who are you, putting yourself before my baby?' A woman spat at her.

Guilt slowed her momentarily, but she had to find her sister and bring her home, that was all she'd allow herself to think about. She smiled grimly as she saw Georgie employ her own elbows to get between two men and reach her side. They linked arms again and continued to push and squeeze through and finally they managed to get inside the door.

'My name is Eliza Morgan and you have my sister here.' She called out, glancing around the chaotic infirmary, unable to determine who were patients and who were doctors. Everyone looked bedraggled and too exhausted to help her.

She walked on, promising God every kind of devotion if only she could find Emily alive and well.

People lay all about in various states of distress, some in beds, some on the floors, others still wandered about looking as lost as she was. It was a dismal scene and she wrinkled her nose against the combined stench of blood, vomit and urine that hung, as thick as fog.

She clenched her fists and marched from room to room calling out for Emily every few minutes. No-one looked at her, but she pressed on, afraid to stop lest she was overcome with grief. If she started to cry now she'd never stop.

How was she going to cope without Ruby to either nod her approval or tilt her head on one side in an, *are you sure?* gesture. With that traitorous thought came Ruby's face, so clear in her mind and so dearly loved.

She scrubbed her hands over her face and looked around. A woman hummed softly as she sat beside a bed, stroking the cheek of a lifeless child.

Eliza blocked her mind to everything but her need to find Emily. She walked along a dimly lit hallway calling out her name and a harassed young man pointed to a door in the corner. She almost cried with frustration as she entered yet another long room and she saw lines of makeshift beds on either side of the room. She gripped Georgie's hand as they slowed their pace and studied every face.

And then, about halfway down the room, on the left-hand side, they saw her. Her lovely face was pale, but unmarked, and was surrounded by a cloud of bedraggled black hair. Georgie burst into tears and ran towards her twin.

Eliza blinked rapidly and followed her. As she reached the bed she bent over and could see the rise and fall of her chest telling her Emily's breathing was steady and deep. Eliza whispered a prayer of thanks and drank in the sight of her sister.

She had no visible injuries to her head or arms, so she gently peeled back the grimy sheet that was covering her and saw that her clothes had been removed and she was wearing a grubby, bloodstained shift that had once belonged to a very much larger woman. She ran her arms gently over her sister's torso and legs and decided the blood had not come from Emily.

'I don't think she's hurt, but she's in a deep sleep.' Georgie nodded and laid her head down beside Emily, her eyes fixed on the face of her twin.

Eliza looked at them and felt relief that they were together, as twins should be. Then she gasped in horror. Twins!

'Georgie, I have to go and tell Aunt Ellie about Ruby, I can't let her hear it from anyone else. Will you feel safe, staying here with Emily?' Georgie nodded.

'Good girl, don't leave her side for anything. I'll come back for you as quickly as I can.'

CHAPTER FOUR

Exiting the infirmary was a great deal easier than entering although the crowd outside was considerably larger, and louder, since she'd arrived.

She retraced her footsteps and arrived, horribly mud splattered, at the entrance of the business that bore the sign *Pargeter and Sons, Apothecary and Perfumiers.*

Eliza's dishevelled appearance and distraught face caused Aunt Ellie to gasp in horror. She put her hands across her mouth. 'Not Ruby?' She moaned.

Eliza nodded, tears welling over. She wrapped her arms around her aunt and both women let themselves go.

'She saved my life, you know.' Aunt Ellie sobbed. 'She was the whole world to me for so long.'

'She saved mine too Aunt Ellie.' Eliza said.

They breathed useless, kind words to each other until they were cried out. As they pulled apart and dabbed their eyes Simon, Ellie's middle son, stepped in and removed his mother's arms from around Eliza.

'You should go back and see what your sister needs.' He told Eliza kindly. 'I'll take care of Mama.'

Eliza nodded gratefully, kissed them both on the cheek and ran back to the infirmary.

This time she was prepared for the melee and nothing delayed her. Her elbows and fists ploughed through the crowd and she was back at the door to the room that housed her sister in no time. Only then did she pause to suck in a deep breath and prepare to face what would come next.

'Hey, you can't loiter about here. Wait downstairs.'

The bullying, almost accusatory tone cut through her self-pity and her Morgan backbone came to the rescue. 'My sister is here, injured. I'm waiting for a doctor to tell me how badly hurt she is.'

'Name?' He barked

'Morgan.' She barked back.

He looked at her with something approaching respect. 'I'll send someone to you, but you'd better be prepared for a wait. They're awful busy, what with the storm damage.'

'I know.'

He nodded once and left her.

She closed her eyes. For the first time in this vile day there was nothing for her to do. Georgie was with Emily. Simon was with Ellie. She'd wait out here, with her memories of Ruby. She ached to see her familiar smile, the one that said, *you can cope, you're built like me.*

Eliza loved being a Morgan woman. They could take on anything they had a mind to, according to Ruby. But she didn't have a mind to take this on, not yet. She'd expected to have many more years learning from Ruby.

As a young girl she'd grown up being told she was responsible for her small sisters. *Go and entertain the twins. Take them for a walk. Get them their supper. Don't let them come to harm. Keep them safe.*

When Mama died, and Papa went away, the three small girls had moved in with Ruby and she'd taken over that burden, giving Eliza the freedom to be her own person. Now the responsibility for the twins had fallen back to her and she'd stepped up, knowing she had no choice.

Brisk footsteps headed her way and she looked up to see a young man rushing along the hallway. He waved out a hand and called out. 'Morgan? Are you Miss Morgan?'

Eliza nodded and straightened her shoulders. Ruby had always advised her to forget what couldn't be changed and focus her energy on what could. Her priority was Emily, so she'd focus on her and take everything one task at a time, see it through to the end then start the next.

'Thank goodness you're here, you can take her home. There's nothing we can do for her and we need the bed.' The man said, not hiding the relief in his voice.

Eliza glared at him angrily. 'You need the bed so you're going to let her go home, in the condition she's in? And how do you suggest I care for her?'

He raised his hands in a gesture of surprise. 'I'm sorry, haven't you already been spoken to?'

'I have not.'

He flushed and shifted his shoulders awkwardly. 'Sorry, we do our best, but...' seeing no sympathy in her face he changed tack.

'She has no evident injuries, you see. We think she's in shock and has simply closed her mind off. I wish she could stay because she's a fascinating case. I'd like to observe her recovery but there's never enough, time or beds!' He smiled, before remembering himself.

He led Eliza into the ward and walked directly to Emily's bed, where he held her wrist for a moment and then laid his hand gently across her brow.

'You can see for yourself, she's calm and unhurt, has no fever and no vomiting. There's nothing we can do for her, I can't justify letting her stay.'

Eliza remained silent, willing him to tell her what to do.

'My advice is take her home and keep her warm. When she wakes give her what she wants, food or drink, and see how she goes.' He saw the fear in her face and softened. 'Take her home, she'll be more comfortable, and you can do as much as us, if not more. She needs you. People here need me, I must put them first.'

The door behind them swung open and a tall man, older and well built, came bursting in on a wave of cold air that smelt like damp wool. He nodded to the doctor - who made a brisk exit - and quickly enveloped Eliza in a hug even as his eyes raked over Emily and Georgie.

'Oh, Uncle Hugh.' Eliza sighed as he wrapped his arms even tighter and held her. She told him everything that had happened in a gush of words, but no more tears.

CHAPTER FIVE

Hugh Daventor squeezed his favourite niece, in a proper hug before gripping her shoulders. He held her at arms-length and gave her an encouraging smile. 'You're having a terrible time but you're not alone. I'll help you to stay strong my girl.'

He turned to the bed and stroked his hand across the mingled hair of Georgie and Emily and caught his breath at their loveliness. The contrast between their delicate, creamy skin and masses of jet black hair always stopped him in his tracks. He remembered Ruby confiding her fears that the twins were too lovely for their own good.

'They've only got to smile and blink their pretty blue eyes and they get what they want. Not from me, but they know every merchant in The Foregate and have made fools of them all. I don't know what's going to become of them, I really don't. They're so sweet and delicate looking but, dear Lord, when they throw a tantrum they're monstrous.'

He turned to Eliza who also watched the twins. She lacked their beauty, but to him, she was the special one. Her hair was a mass of coppery curls that sprang about with a life of their own and her cheeks had a healthy glow, everything about her spoke of energy and life. Her remarkable green eyes met his and he swallowed quickly. Her likeness to Ruby was staggering.

'They say she's not hurt, just badly shocked. She was trapped beneath… we don't know how long for. They think she'll be better off in familiar surroundings so they want me to take her home, but I'm not sure how to manage it.

'We walked here, Georgie and me, through The Foregate, but the track is gone, washed away and no-one will allow me to drive a hired carriage along there.'

'We'll manage.' He said.

A doctor, older than the one Eliza had spoken to earlier, approached them and Hugh pulled him to one side. 'I need help getting the girl to my carriage, can you spare two men?'

The doctor nodded, he couldn't, but getting rid of this group would free up much needed space.

Soon, and with minimal fuss, two porters gently lifted Emily into a carriage that had been brought right to the door. Georgie climbed in beside her and the carriage headed for home with Hugh and Eliza walking beside it.

'The horses will have enough work to do navigating the mud and I'd welcome a stretch.' He'd declared, and she agreed.

They linked arms and he encouraged her to lean on him for the walk.

'I chatted with the doctor, and you're correct. They're certain Emily is not injured physically, but they don't understand this state that she's in.

Eliza shook her head. 'I'm afraid of what might happen if I don't look after her the way I should.'

He barked out a laugh. 'So are they, I suspect, which is why they've encouraged us to get her home. Now then, that fellow I was just speaking with seems to be an able chap. He's promised to call on you every now and again until she wakes, at which time, hopefully, she'll tell us what she needs.'

He looked at her white face, jaw firmly clenched and eyes swimming with unshed tears.

'Don't spend your time fearing the worst, my dear. It's hard, but you must trust that the worst has happened, and things will improve. Be strong and do what you can.'

The carriage jolted to a halt and Hugh stepped to the door. 'I'll carry her in, you go ahead and show me where to go. Georgie, get out of my way girl, I can't carry both of you.'

He carried Emily up to her own bed and within minutes Georgie was curled up beside her, fast asleep.

'They're both settled, you need to do the same.' Hugh told her. 'I've got to go and see about some damage we've sustained at home and you've done enough for today. Try to rest, I'll call on you tomorrow and we'll face it together.'

Eliza closed the door behind him and he allowed his shoulders to slump. Bright and vibrant Ruby was dead, and the pain he felt was worse than any he'd ever experienced.

He sent his carriage ahead. 'Wait for me at the bridge, I'll walk through town.' He wanted time to remember her and to keep his grief private.

CHAPTER SIX

Eliza spent a desperate night pacing between the little chair in Ruby's room that she'd claimed, and the sleeping twins. She'd only managed to doze as dawn broke and had woken up with a thick head and a sore back.

And now she was faced with family, in the form of Aunt Ellie and Uncle Hugh, who'd followed one another into the house that morning - Ellie armed with food and questions - Hugh with paperwork and calm.

Two hours after their arrival Eliza wished them both gone. They were not natural friends, only linked by love and respect for Ruby. Aunt Ellie was always a little awestruck and fluttery around Hugh and he found her silliness a trial.

They danced around each other now and Eliza wanted to scream. She rubbed her throbbing temples and tried not to snap as the same questions, phrased a dozen different ways, were repeated.

'I don't understand why they went out in such terrible weather.' Aunt Ellie wailed, almost as though having someone to blame would make things easier. Eliza patted the back of the older woman's hand and looked in desperation to Hugh.

He walked to the table and untied the bundle of paperwork. 'Ellie my dear, there's no point in continuing in this line, it's upsetting us all. We must accept what has happened and look ahead.'

Aunt Ellie opened her mouth to argue and Eliza felt a pang for her. She must be distraught at the loss of her sister, but her habit of making a meal of any situation made her hard to love sometimes.

Hugh tapped the floor with his cane. 'Let's end this questioning and second guessing. We all know that once Ruby's mind was made up nothing could change it. Come and sit at the table, all of you. We have business to discuss.'

He briskly ran through the arrangements that Ruby had made, in the event of her death.

'You'll have an income, but not a great one. The running of Ruby's affairs now transfers to Messrs Givens so there's no need for you to worry on that matter.'

He laid his hand on the bigger pile of papers. 'I'll leave this paperwork with you. Whenever you feel ready you can look through it.

'An allowance will be made automatically and should cover your living expenses. We can go over things together at any time and if changes need to be made they can be. I'll always be here for you my dear, so if things get too much speak up.'

He slid the pile of papers across the table towards Eliza who nodded dully, she hadn't thought any further ahead than getting through this day.

He turned to Ellie. 'Come my dear, let me see you home.'

'Oh no, we can't leave them here.' Aunt Ellie protested. 'No really, three girls alone in this house won't do. They'll have to move in with me.'

Without thinking for a second Eliza shook her head. 'No. We're staying here.'

Aunt Ellie sniffed. 'You're no more than a child. You need to be taken care of and I shall do that. For my sister. She put her hands over her heart and looked upwards.'

Eliza scowled and glared at Hugh, but he shook his head, wanting no part of this fight.

'I insist the three of you come and live with me.' Aunt Ellie stated firmly. 'We'll be a squeeze, but we're family and we'll manage. I'm quite sure that's what Ruby would advise us to do.'

Eliza very much doubted Ruby would advise any such thing and anyway, she'd decided they were staying here. 'It's kind of you to offer your home to us Aunt Ellie, and I'm grateful, truly I am. But this is our home.'

Her aunt dissolved into tears and Eliza wrapped her arms around her, sorry for her pain and hating that she was causing her more.

'I'm of age and it's for me to stand up and take care of us. And we won't be alone, Mary and Juliet are here with us. Jackson is only next door if a man's help is needed.'

'Companions and gardeners!' Aunt Ellie howled. 'When you have family nearby, oh no Eliza, I can't allow this.'

Eliza bit her lip and saved her energy, having already decided that no power on earth would persuade her to leave Ruby's house. It represented everything that had been good and safe in her world, and it was a place she would make safe and good again. There was nothing to argue about.

'Eliza dear, my mind is made up.' Aunt Ellie spoke as sharply as she could.

Eliza bent and kissed her aunt's hot, damp cheek. 'Mine is also. We're staying here, so please don't fuss. We'll see you every day if you wish. Uncle Hugh, tell us what you think?' She challenged him directly.

'Three girls living alone would be inadvisable ordinarily, but Mary and Juliet are as good as family and would fight like tigers to protect them. I'm also reminded of the doctor fellow yesterday who said Emily would do best in familiar surroundings. I'm afraid she has us beaten Ellie.'

Aunt Ellie bit her lip and dabbed at her eyes.

Eliza tried to reassure her. 'I know how to run this house, I've managed the accounts for years now, and I feel safe here. I felt this house wrap itself around me when I first came here. I felt protected then and I still feel that way. No harm will come to us here, I know it.'

Aunt Ellie sighed, her face grey and defeated, 'I can't argue with you tonight. We'll talk again tomorrow.'

Hugh helped Ellie to her feet but kept his eyes on Eliza. 'I would say I don't know where you get that stubborn streak from, but that would be a lie. You're so much like her it's uncanny. Just don't be too proud to ask for help if you struggle with anything. We're your family and will do anything we can to help you.'

She nodded, but he wasn't going to let it go that easily. He stepped towards her and took both her hands in his and shook them gently.

'I'm serious, I want you to promise me that the pride you've no doubt inherited along with her stubbornness won't impede you. I want you to come to me if you feel daunted at any time. Now, promise me.'

'I promise, Uncle Hugh, truly I do.' She'd grown up witnessing the genuine friendship between Ruby and Hugh and was thankful beyond words that he was nearby. But for now, she wanted them all gone so that she could be alone with her sisters.

CHAPTER SEVEN

The following morning Eliza stretched and realised that she felt hungry, in fact she couldn't remember the last meal she ate. The last two days had been grindingly hard, fear and sadness almost defeating her, even as she dealt with well-intentioned callers.

Before heading down stairs she looked in on the twins who lay side by side in bed, as she'd left them the night before. The only difference between them was the colour in their cheeks and the gloss of their hair.

Emily slept but Georgie opened her eyes and looked at Eliza before burying her face in her twin's shoulder.

Eliza bent and stroked her hair, wondering how on earth she would manage these two when they were back to normal, refusing to contemplate any other outcome.

She made for the kitchen. A hot meal would set her up, then she'd feel clearer in her mind.

Normally, she'd expect the kitchen to be warm and noisy, the shutters would be flung wide open and the fire would be roaring. Mary would be clattering the pans and humming as she cooked.

But not today. The air was sour and the light dim. She could see Juliet on her knees, clumsily trying to get the fire started. 'You shouldn't be doing that, where's Mary?'

Juliet shrugged, 'I banged on her door and she told me to bugger off.'

Eliza got to her knees and pushed Juliet aside. 'Here, let me try.' She stacked the paper and layered the kindling and sat back on her heels to wait, as the tiny flame flickered.

'There, that should take now.' She wiped her hands on her dress. 'Don't put any more on it until that flame's a bit stronger. I'll go up and see where Mary is.'

She ran up the stairs and hammered on Mary's bedroom door then, getting no reply, walked right in, a thing she'd never done before.

'Mary?'

The huddled mound under the blanket didn't move so she crossed the room and threw open the shutters and then the window, letting in a breath-taking gust of icy wind which smelt a great deal sweeter than the stagnant air around Mary's bed.

She turned and firmly tugged the blanket, exposing Mary's top half.

'Leave me alone.' The woman groaned. 'And shut the bloody window before you go, it's freezing in here.'

'Get up and light a fire if you're cold!' Eliza sat down heavily on the end of the bed, forcing Mary to give her space or suffer a broken foot.

Mary hauled herself up on one elbow, her face tired and pale, showing all the pain she was feeling. Eliza's heart went out to her, but she couldn't let her slip away.

'I've got Georgie refusing to leave Emily's side, Juliet trying to light a fire and almost burning the house down and now you, hiding up here doing bugger all.' Eliza first time of cursing tasted quite sweet.

She leaned back on Mary's narrow bed and wriggled herself into a more comfortable spot. 'If mooning about and doing nothing is good enough for you, it'll be good enough for me. I'm not taking care of you all.'

'Leave me alone!' Mary pleaded, her face screwed up and her fists clenched. 'And don't curse.'

Eliza clenched her jaw and shook her head. 'I can't run this house and manage those two without your help, so we either get on with it together or we stay here.'

Mary shook her head. 'I can't. I've had enough, Ruby was everything to me, we shared everything, and we were always there for each other. Nothing was half as important as Ruby was to me. I don't want to go on without her.'

Eliza put her arms around the older woman and rubbed her back until she felt the passion of her grief ease. 'I know, and I'm so sorry for you, but truly Mary, I need you.'

Mary gathered herself and brushed her tears away. 'You can manage if you put your mind to it. You're cut from the same cloth as her, she knew it as well as I did, she was proud of you.'

'Tell me about her, about the days before we came along?'

Mary talked, awkwardly at first. Her words and the stories were a jumble of tears and smiles, a tangle of love and loss.

When Mary quietened, Eliza talked, and they shared memories of the woman they'd both loved. Gradually, as the sun warmed the air, an understanding was forged between them.

Mary drew herself upright. 'Go on, give me space to get dressed and I'll get on with some food. I'll do what I can to get you through. I'm doing for her though, not you.'

'Thank you. I can't imagine what I'd do without you. I don't know what to do or where to turn.'

Mary looked at her and the ghost of smile crossed her face. 'You'll do what needs doing, one day at a time. I'll be behind you for as long as you need me.'

'I'll always need you.'

'We'll be at loggerheads in weeks missy. But we'll get through, you'll see.'

CHAPTER EIGHT

MARY

Me and Ruby had been pals for forty years and let me tell you, you don't get over a loss like that in a hurry. It knocked me about something cruel, still does when I think of it. I forget, and then I look up to tell her something, the pain takes my breath away.

We met as fourteen years olds with nothing but what we stood up in. I'd just started working at the inn, I served the ale and flirted with the customers, as I'd expected to. It was a shock when I learned the other part of my job to keep the gaffer's bed warm, but I did it.

Folks hereabouts were quick to look down on girls like me, but let me tell you, he took better care of me than my bleeding Ma ever did, even if he was a miserable bastard some days.

I close my eyes and I can see Ruby now. She stood in the corner of the inn looking like a cornered fox, as skinny as you like, but with a belly on her that couldn't be hidden. I could see her shaking from across the room, but she stuck her chin out and I warmed to her. I knew how she felt and I recognised the guts it took to stand there, dry eyed. I don't know why, but I wanted to help her. I dragged her out of the way of the grabbing hands and gave her some food.

We both made a friend that night.

She was on her way to Ma's for work, so we could only manage to meet every so often, but I looked forward to those times. She made my life brighter, it was like being closer to the sun when I was with her. The first time I ever laughed was with her, and once we started we never stopped. She showed me what happiness was and I can't put a price on that. And she had some spirit, she accepted where she was, but never accepted it was where she'd stay. She never stopped dreaming.

When those fellows said she was dead I took to my bed for the first time in my life and if I'd had my way it would have been the last, but Eliza was having none of it. I looked up, all ready to chuck the cheeky little bitch out on her ear, and I saw young Ruby looking at me again, scared to death and too stubborn to cry.

I had no choice, I had to get up and help.

But those first few weeks were a struggle with no Ruby to keep us going and everyone running around trying to do the best for poor little Emily.

Georgie stayed by her side, but she's no use if there's anything to be done, so me, Eliza and Juliet, took it in turns to sit and watch over the pair of them around the clock.

Thank God Eliza was with her the first time she stirred for the shock would have killed me. I'd written her off as dead. I'd have cut out my tongue before admitting it, but I expected to hear her last breath every blasted day.

She's awake now, but she's not right. She eats a bit, but not enough to keep a body alive, but that's not the worst of it. Once she started wakening up it ruined her night sleep. She'd lain there, as peaceful as you like for weeks, but now she thrashes about and screams like the devil every night and none of us can rest.

The doctors say she'll improve, but how the hell do they know that? Lying bastards, they tell you what'll shut you up.

She gets up for an hour or so every day and sits at the table and you'd think that would make the house a happier place, but now they're not so worried about Emily, it seems Eliza and Georgie can't be in the same room without fighting like cats, tearing strips of each other.

That, and the lack of sleep is getting the better of me. I'm not their kin and I'm not their servant. I had to sit Eliza down and tell her to get her head out from her arse or she'd be doing her own cooking and cleaning.

CHAPTER NINE

Eliza slammed out of the house in such a temper she didn't stop to grab her cloak. She marched along The Foregate in a seething fury. Who the hell did Mary think she was? Lecturing her as though she were a child.

She was weary, sleeping in the same room as the twins at night was hard. Since Emily had woken up she'd fallen victim to horrendous nightmares which were so upsetting that Georgie became almost hysterical watching her. Between the two of them Eliza hadn't slept through the night for weeks and was barely functioning.

She didn't know what to do with Juliet, who seemed to spend her life lurking about trying to help, but only succeeding in getting in her way.

In blind panic Eliza suggested she spend each morning in the kitchen helping Mary out. On the second morning, the two of them had an almighty fight and now both women were threatening to leave.

Tempers had not been soothed when the butcher refused to let them have meat because a payment had been overlooked. Eliza listened as Mary told him that he'd see no more business from them and he'd laughed, 'No matter lover, I'd sooner supply folks that pays their dues.'

Eliza marched on, self-righteously muttering to herself about the ignorance and ingratitude of others and before she knew it she was standing in front of the cathedral, dashing away tears of frustration. The strenuous walk had released her tension and she admitted to herself that Mary's words had stung because they were true. Blast the woman!

She didn't want her or Juliet to leave, they'd been a part of her family since she'd arrived at seven years of age and she loved them both.

Mary had been Ruby's friend, but when Eliza and her sisters had been orphaned she took care of them until Ruby found Juliet. She moved in as a companion and tutor to the girls and they'd practically grown up together.

Ruby would have kept the two women with her come what may and Eliza had even more reason to do so. She needed their protection if she was to be allowed to remain in the house with her sisters. Moving in with Aunt Ellie would be a stifling disaster, and she'd do whatever it took to prevent that happening.

But the money question worried her. The butcher this morning was not the first to demand money. She'd been responsible for the household accounts for a long time and she knew how much was outstanding.

Ruby had refused to be completely open, presumably through some misguided idea of protecting her. She'd been settling what she could as and when, but if word got out that they were struggling she'd have creditors hounding her mercilessly.

Her pace picked up as random thoughts raced through her brain. Mary wanted to be left alone to run the house her way. Juliet needed to be occupied usefully. Georgie was fractious and awkward and poor Emily needed to be cared for. It was up to Eliza to find a solution for them all.

She turned her back on the Severn and headed thoughtfully away, going down the gentle slope towards the little row of houses and small shops of Sidbury where she'd spent the first seven years of her life, surrounded by warmth, love, and security.

Facing her demons in the old family home was something she'd avoided doing for years. But losing Ruby gave her no choice. She was an adult, and as Mary had so bluntly told her, it was time she started to act like one.

She spent an hour strolling around, looking at the new buildings that had sprung up and playing with ideas. She watched people going about their business and kept a close eye on the class of carriage that passed her by on their way to and from London.

The tiny hamlet was bustling, far busier than she remembered and, by the time she turned for home she'd got the seeds of a plan brewing. She stopped off in The Foregate, where she spent a productive hour with her aunt before returning home.

'Where have you been?' Georgie wailed when Eliza walked in. 'I imagined you dead like Ruby. I've been watching for you for hours.'

Eliza felt a quick pang of guilt, but Mary, hearing her, shot out a response. 'Don't you try that missy, I told you she was out for a walk and you were perfectly happy until she stepped through the door. Bloody play acting.'

'Does she listen to us all the time?' Georgie hissed to Eliza.

'Only when I must.' Mary replied, slamming the kitchen door and sending a draft through the house.

Eliza laughed and took her sister's arm. 'We need to talk Georgie, come and sit with me while I tell you more.'

Georgie looked up, but with little interest. 'What?'

'I'm afraid we're going to lose everything, including Mary and Juliet if we don't make some adjustments. It's not your fault, it's mine. I've been marking time, as though I've been waiting for Ruby to come back. But I can't do that any longer.

'We have no money and I need to find out why, in the meantime we need to earn money and we need to stop fighting. This is our life and we have to pull together to make it a happy one'

Georgie was still listening and looking nervous.

'We have some uncomfortable choices to make and I'm going to need your help. I want to start by altering our sleeping arrangements. When Emily suffers a nightmare, you make the situation far worse by crying along with her. I'll allow Emily all the time and help she needs to recover but I'm not listening to you whining like a kicked puppy.'

Georgie pouted, but Eliza fixed her with a warning stare and the threatened tears didn't fall.

'I understand it frightens you to see her that way, but you make it almost impossible for me, that can't go on. I've decided we need you to have a separate space.'

Georgie shook her head vehemently. 'But we've never slept apart.'

'And I'm not suggesting you do now so take that sulky look off your face and listen before you start complaining. Emily can't help the way she is, but you can. I'm sick of our constant falling out and you must be too. Let me say it all then you can go away and cry over it all at once and have done with it. But make no mistake, things are going to change.'

Georgie's shoulders slumped, but she offered no more argument. 'You're worse than Ruby, what other changes?'

Eliza straightened her shoulders. 'Bedrooms first. We need to clear out Ruby's rooms so the three of us can move in to them. You two can share the bigger room and I'll take the smaller one. When Emily has a nightmare, I can sit with her and you can crawl into my bed. She'll quieten much more quickly that way and you won't be so upset if you don't stay to see her torment. We'll move Ruby's things into my room.'

Georgie twisted her hair around her finger and looked away. A pretty ploy Eliza had often seen her use and it fell on stony ground this time.

Georgie stiffened. 'It really scares me when she gets like that, do you think she always will?'

Eliza rubbed her aching temples and sighed. 'I don't know. I don't know anything, I'm trying my best, that's all.'

Georgie nodded. 'Having the bigger rooms would be better for us, but I don't see why we should do the moving. Can't you tell Mary and Juliet to move our things?'

Eliza pressed her fingers to her lips for a moment and paused. 'That's the other thing. Mary is Ruby's friend, not a servant. She'll stay with us and continue to cook and clean as she always has, but she's not ever to be treated as anything but a member of the family. She's never been other than a good friend to us and we must treat her with due respect or she'll go.'

Georgie looked shocked. 'Mary couldn't leave us.'

Eliza walked over to the window and peered out before closing the shutters. 'She could actually, and if we don't take better care of her, I'm afraid she will. She's very sad you know.'

Georgie's shoulders shook. 'Everything's gone wrong and I hate it, I want Emily back.'

Eliza nodded but made no move to hug her sister. 'I want Ruby back, but it's not going to happen is it? Be thankful that you don't have to live without Emily, she's different, but you still have her. What she needs is for us to build a routine around her so that she feels secure and can sense that we're all safe. Doctor Haskins says a few months of peace and rest and she'll start to get back to normal. She's not going to die you know.'

Georgie wiped her face and tried to smile. 'She's really not going to die?'

'Not yet, I can promise you that.'

Georgie nodded. 'What else have I got to do to help you?'

'Good girl, come on, we'll sort out the bedrooms now and I'll tell you the rest as we work. It's not good for us to be sitting about doing nothing every day, so we're going to work. I'm going to open Ruby's lending library for three days a week. It seems like a good place for me to start. Now, start piling these papers into that trunk.'

'You said we! What work am I supposed to do?'

The panic in Georgie's voice was very real and Eliza smiled. 'Ah well, you're the lucky one because you have a choice. Aunt Ellie needs some help at Madame Eloise and she's prepared to train you.'

She closed the lid of the trunk and turned to another bundle of paper, old and yellowed, crackling with age. 'Hmm, I should probably go through all of this one day.' She muttered.

Georgie had been sitting on her heels looking dazed. 'I have to go and work with Aunt Ellie?' She put her head on one side, as though waiting for Eliza to laugh.

'If that doesn't appeal to you, then you must stay here and help Juliet. She doesn't know it yet, but she's going to pay her own way by tutoring students in the school room downstairs. Which, by the way, you'll be helping me prepare.'

Eliza ignored Georgie's shocked face and continued calmly. 'I've thought it all through, we're living beyond our means and this seems like an ideal solution. Mary and Juliet will be here all day every day, so Emily will never be left alone. You know how much she loves Juliet, she'll be perfectly happy sitting in her classroom.

'Ruby always worked and made it clear that we would too, this may not be what she had in mind but it's the best that I can come up with. I believe we're secure in this house, but we have to earn our own living.'

CHAPTER TEN

Eliza smiled encouragingly as she and Georgie left home together a few day later.

She was dressed sensibly in a sturdy dress that she used when doing the housework, she had her stout boots on and her hair was scraped out of sight under an old bonnet.

Georgie had been up for hours and had taken great pains to dress appropriately. She wore a pale pink gown which was trimmed with cream lace and had a delicate shawl of a deeper pink around her shoulders. Her hair style looked very complicated and was slightly drooping already, and her scowl could sour milk.

Eliza ignored the thumping behind her eyes and tried not to take her own nerves out on Georgie. 'You'll love it if only you give it a chance, and it's not like you have much choice, it's this or teaching.'

Georgie shuddered. 'It's having to go out to work at all that I hate.' She started to whine but backed down quickly as she saw Eliza's white face.

'I know I'm the lucky one. You'll be stuck in that dreary library with nothing but books. You'll be in tears of boredom by noon. I'm Aunt Ellie's favourite so I expect we'll sit and drink hot chocolate for much of the day.'

The sisters kissed, and Georgie entered the doorway to Madame Eloise, leaving Eliza to walk on and consider the success of her actions of the past week.

Filling Ruby's place at the library was the logical thing for her to do and once she'd reached that decision, it was a small task to convince Aunt Ellie to give Georgie work.

Juliet had been overjoyed when she'd mentioned the idea of a small school room. Teaching was her passion after all. She'd confessed that much as she loved being a companion to them, she dearly missed teaching. Now she could have the best of both worlds.

She cheerfully worked alongside Eliza transforming their neglected old school room into something more up to date. She knew exactly where everything was to be placed and quickly took over the task.

Mary hadn't commented on the changing arrangements, but her nod of approval was encouragement enough.

The one thing Eliza hadn't done was allow herself any thinking time. She feared an attack of the miseries, and there was far too much to be done. This day was presenting enough of a challenge as it was.

The cathedral loomed before her and it was with some regret that she ignored the grassy path that led down towards the river, in favour of turning left.

At the bottom of the slope where the ground levelled out sat her destination, the smart house that used to be her childhood home, but that Ruby had converted into a lending library for the city.

She glanced up at the shuttered windows and almost turned away, doubting her ability to go in. This was the test. She hadn't entered the building last week, nerves getting the better of her but now… Well, she couldn't turn tail and go home, she needed to be strong for everyone else. And re-opening the library was her choice, she wanted to be the one to keep Ruby's dream alive.

She stepped forward and pulled out the heavy key, ready to unlock the door. Not thinking, just breathing.

'Are you opening up again love?'

Eliza started. A tall, slender woman, a good ten years her senior was smiling down at her. She was dressed exquisitely, although her voice didn't have the twang of grandeur that Georgie and Aunt Ellie tried to emulate. This woman came from working stock and didn't try to hide it.

Eliza managed to nod a yes, but her throat was full of unshed tears and she dared not speak.

'That's good to know. It's been missed, and it'll give you something to do while you work things out.'

Eliza looked at the woman blankly, certain they'd never met and yet the stranger had breezed in confidently and was clearly at home as she unhesitatingly flung open a window, sending a beam of light over the swirling dust.

'Don't mind me now, you get yourself sorted. I know what needs doing in here.' She nodded encouragingly before throwing open the rest of the shutters.

Eliza couldn't allow this pushy woman to distract her. She'd decided that her responsibility was to be here, in Ruby's place, so facing down her demons was her priority, anything else could wait.

She circled the ground floor, determined to withstand the blow after blow of painful memories that swept through her. She had to sweep her childish fears away if she was to lead her sisters safely into the future.

Memory guided her feet to what had been Papa's study, she inhaled deeply, was there still a hint of his tobacco in the air or was that wishful thinking? She moved on to the room where she had her lessons with Ann and she smiled, it seemed an impossibly small space to her now. She peered through the window as she remembered doing most days, staring across the courtyard to watch the door to the newspaper offices, waiting for Papa to head home.

Having completed a circuit of the ground floor she headed up the stairs. At the top of the flight she turned automatically to sit in the bay window and let her mind go back to the last time she'd sat here.

Papa had asked her to find Mama and she'd raced off, delighted to be given a chance to please him. She slipped on her new shoes, hoping her spoilt little sisters would envy her for having them, but they hadn't even noticed.

She skipped from room to room, peering under beds and flinging open cupboards, but there was no sign of Mama. She called out once, twice and then once more, before running downstairs to Papa's study. 'She's not here, I've looked everywhere.'

He swept her up in his arms and kissed her cheek before setting her down on the floor. 'Keep an eye on the twins for me, try to stop them killing each other, there's my best girl, I'll find Mama.'

He patted the top of her head and was gone.

Papa's footsteps rebounded on the wooden floors above, his voice getting louder each time he called and got no response. His boots cracked sharply on the wooden treads as he pounded back downstairs and out through the front door.

She ran back upstairs and crawled into the big window, from where she could see the entire courtyard. Papa strode out, shouting at the top of his voice and she knew something was badly wrong. Other men, bearing flaming torches, stood around him listening as he spoke urgently.

The twins played in the room behind her, a shriek from one was followed by a giggle from the other. Eliza curled over the horrid cramp in her tummy and tried not to cry, they were so sweet and silly, and she felt sorry that they would soon know the desperate fear that she felt.

The torches outside shifted and separated as the searching men fanned out across the ground covering a huge area. They kept in touch with each other by means of high pitched whistles.

Her stomach cramped again when frantic shouts broke out and she pressed her nose to the glass. She'd sniffed and blinked her eyes rapidly as she whispered, 'Our Father', trying hard to be a big girl.

The flames drew together and all she could see was a hovering ball of fire. The torches shifted again and became a line heading back to the house.

She saw Ben and Joseph carrying Mama, and behind them, Papa, with Thomas in his arms.

.

CHAPTER ELEVEN

Eliza heard footsteps on the wooden stairs and hastily wiped away her tears.

'Ah bless you. I don't blame you for having a weep, the sad memories this place must hold and you only just losing Ruby. Come on down now though. I'll stand guard while you tidy up your face and hair. Go on lovey, one good cry is enough.'

Eliza did as she was told and as she doused her face in icy water she gave herself a talking to. She'd faced it and got through it, she simply could not give in to tears again. There was no point, this was her life and she must make the most of it. She straightened her shoulders and walked back into the library, head held high.

The woman was waiting for her and she gave Eliza an approving nod. 'That's better, now you look ready for the world. Feeling stronger?'

'Yes, thank you. You've been very kind, I don't think we've met, did you know Ruby?'

The woman smiled broadly. 'I certainly did. She was Ma's best friend and when Ma died she became my best friend. You don't know me, but I know you Eliza. Ruby was that proud of you. She loved the twins, of course, but you meant everything to her. I hope you know that?'

Eliza nodded tearfully.

The woman gave her quick squeeze. 'Well, don't worry about what you do, or don't know. I'm Ana, and I've been coming here for years, one day a week to spend the morning with Ruby, and I should like to do the same with you. That'll give us all the time we need to get to know each other, a bit at a time.'

Eliza nodded. 'I'd like that. I don't seem to have my wits about me today, but I would like to talk to you.'

Ana frowned slightly. 'Is this the first time you've been here, since…?'

Without waiting for a response Ana sniffed. 'Might have been better to have brought someone with you, a bit of support.'

'Yes.' Eliza said weakly.

'Sit down, I'll be back.' Ana ordered, heading for the door.

Eliza dropped into the seat gratefully. Ordinarily she'd have resisted doing what she was told to do, but today she was thankful for it.

Her new friend returned carrying a steaming coffee pot in one hand and an aromatic paper parcel in the other, both of which she set on a table with a thump, before bending to open a small door in a cupboard and lift out two thick cups. These she set down on the table and filled to the brim with the contents of the jug.

'Drink this and then have a bite out of that.' She ripped open the package to release the steam from a fresh meat pie and pushed it towards Eliza.

'Go on,' she nodded. 'Eat it. Jon Bowers wouldn't sell me rubbish, he's been trying to get on my good side for years. He tried getting on Ruby's good side for longer mind, but she …'

She slapped her mouth shut. 'Never mind all that now, eat.'

The first mouthful of coffee stole her breath away, she coughed and turned watery eyes to Ana. 'That's not just coffee?'

'No! It's got a drop of brandy in it. French, he reckons. Mind you, he always was a bloody liar.'

She smiled and drank her own, smacking her lips with pleasure. 'Either way, it'll brace you. Ruby was a help to me when I needed a friend, and now I'll be a friend to you.'

Eliza's eyes smarted, she'd never needed a friend before and was touched when Ana leant forward and patted her on the cheek.

'Do you have anybody you can talk to? I only ask because when my Ma died I needed to talk about her.

'I'd sit here for hour upon hour telling Ruby stuff she already knew and she never tired of listening.

'Why don't you drink down the rest of that while it's hot and I'll sit beside you for an hour or two, that way, if you need to talk you'll have a set of ears handy?'

Softened by the brandy, and warmed by the kindness of this stranger, Eliza let her feeling flood out. 'It's all confused in my head. Mama and Papa and Ruby.'

Ana nodded. 'Don't try to make sense of it, just get it all out. We can fill in the gaps later.'

'I can't recall how I felt when Mama died because Papa walked out on the three of us the next morning and it was the loss of him that broke my heart. I've never stopped waiting for him to come back.

'I always knew she loved us and would have stayed with us if she could, but he could have stayed, and chose not to, and I wish I knew why. I loved him more than I loved her you see. The twins were Ma's pets, they needed all her time and so I turned to Pa.'

Ana's kind eyes watched her, but she said nothing.

Eliza took a gulping breath. 'After they both went, the twins still had each other. I had no-one, and I thought it was because I wasn't special enough to make him stay.

'Ruby came then, and she taught me to be proud of who I was and told me I was never to think that I'd driven him away. And I had thought that, I was the grown up one, and if I couldn't make him want to stay, then the lack must be mine.

'Ruby got me through by showing me, every day that I was as good as anyone, and better than many. I watched her as she worked and how she managed her business and I admired her so much. She never once made me feel as though we were in her way. Her love was unconditional.'

She watched as Ana upended the jug of coffee, sharing the last few dregs equally between them.

'She healed me. She talked to me and made me question everything. She encouraged me to read the newspaper and to pay attention to what was around me. She listened to my childish thoughts and convinced me to think events out more fully and to try to see what was between the lines, not to take anything at face value.'

She smiled guiltily. 'I was envious of the twins' prettiness, they sparkled in company and everyone admired them. I was overlooked, being plain and quiet and I used to cry about that, but Ruby made me realise that I had something special. She said that every time they were complimented I should agree and be thankful, because my quick brain was the greater gift.'

Eliza's voice faltered. 'I don't think I can manage without her.'

Ana leaned forward and took her chin in her hands. 'You can, because she taught you how. It might take you a while to trust yourself, but you'll get there.'

They sat together quietly, sipping the last of the coffee and when it was gone Eliza set her cup down and stood up. 'Can you stay for another hour? I want to go and say hello to John and Jacob, the newspaper men. I haven't visited them for years.'

Ana flapped her hands in a gesture of dismissal and Eliza darted out of the back door and crossed the courtyard.

Returning to the house had unearthed sad memories, but out here was different. Out here had been a happy place to be a little girl, she smiled and hung on to that thought.

CHAPTER TWELVE

The women of Worcester had taken Madame Eloise and her treatments to their hearts, and Ellie was usually kept busy all day and on through the evenings.

Since Hannah had left her - for the country and a new husband – she'd struggled to find a replacement. One disappointment after another led her to decide she'd be better continuing alone. Her hope was that in the fullness of time her younger son, Matty might take over.

The other two had no interest, Sam was fixed on the law and was studying in London while Si was following his father's path and was now the proprietor of Pargeters.

When Eliza had proposed that she take Georgie under her wing she'd jumped at the chance to work with a girl from her own family, it was almost as good as having a daughter of her own. She'd spent the intervening days happily planning how Georgie's training would progress.

Georgie's sweet dreams of hot chocolate and cosy gossiping were trampled to dust minutes after her arrival.

'You're overdressed for the day I have planned for you but there's no time for you to go home and get changed. If you're particularly careful that gown may not get too badly damaged, but you might think about wearing your plain blue tomorrow. Sensible and discreet is our aim. We must never outshine our ladies.'

Georgie face fell, and Ellie smiled grimly. Her first lesson was to teach the girl that Madame Eloise and Aunt Ellie were worlds apart.

'Tell me, what do you know of the history of Madame Eloise?' Ellie asked.

'Um, nothing really.'

'Hmm, well you'll pick it up as we work if you pay attention. I must say, I admire you girls very much for getting out in the world and making your own way. It marks you out as Morgan's.' She sniffed. 'As does your sister's stubborn refusal to move in with me. Follow me.'

Georgie followed obediently all morning, as she tripped up and down the stairs, meeting clients and mixing up her potions.

'Aunt Ellie can I …'

Ellie quickly put her hand up. 'I'm Madame when we're here, it's vital that we maintain a professional distance. Now, come and watch me with this next client. She suffers terribly from thinning hair, which is something I see a lot of, and I'm rather pleased with my treatment.'

'Will you tell me some of the history, Madame?' Georgie asked later, when they squeezed a moment between clients to rest.

Ellie smiled at her lovely niece. She'd worked hard without complaint all morning, she looked tired but there was no hint of a sulk. 'I'd love to blow the dust off my old storied dear. My boys aren't interested in them. I was younger than you are now when I was lucky enough to work as maid for a truly beautiful woman. They were a well to do family and had me trained to keep her looking lovely.

'I had French hairdressers teaching me their tricks, and once, there was a woman who came all the way from Italy to show me how to mix up some of the potions I still use today. It was a wonderful time, almost like playing, some days.

'But time passed, and things changed. There was a row, the why's and the wherefores don't matter. I was put out. No work, no home and no character, all I could do was run to Ruby. We hadn't seen each other for years, but she took me in without hesitation and helped me to set this place up. Her money and my skills.'

A tinkling bell ended the story and Madame and her apprentice headed out to meet their next client.

Later, as they closed for the day Madame became Aunt Ellie again and hugged Georgie close. 'It's been a treat for me to have you here today. I keep a distance between me and my ladies naturally, and of course the same applies to the girls I've had here helping me. To have someone I love and trust to chat with as we work has been wonderful. I spend so much time with my boys I'd forgotten how nice it is to relax with another woman.' She kissed her soundly on the cheek and watched her walk away.

Georgie could do well at Madame Eloise.

CHAPTER THIRTEEN

MARY

What a change I could see in Eliza and Georgie after their first day at work.

Georgie came in like something the cat had finished with, her hair was flattened, her hands were red and that pink gown she'd insisted on wearing was beyond any repairs I could offer, but she was lively and that pleased with herself I could only sit and watch.

She started off lecturing us on how we should walk about with a smile on our own face or the worry lines would fix themselves permanently. Said she wanted a mirror hung in every room to remind us all.

'Madame says it's a habit that should be quashed, those frown lines will get deeper and one day you'll wake up and they'll be there forever.'

That was when we learned that Ellie likes to be called Madame when she struts about her empire. I'll save that little gem up for when I see her round the market, I might even toss a curtsey her way.

'Madame never had to live with you, though did she?' I said. 'That's what caused the lines on my face girl and all the smiling in the world won't shift them. Ground in deep they are.'

I saw Eliza smile.

She asked her if she had to call her Madame all the time, and Georgie says 'yes we like to be addressed as Madame and Georgiana when we're at Madame Eloise. It's important that our ladies see us as professionals.'

Me and Eliza couldn't look at each other.

I sent up a prayer of thanks though. I never doubted that Eliza would come good, she's made of strong stuff. It was Georgie that had me worried. She's so high strung and this business with Emily has changed her, she's not settled in herself, not really.

One day she's high and the next low. I don't know what we'd have done with her if she hadn't stuck with the day's work... but she did!

As for Eliza, she didn't say much. Her eyes were swollen, but she had a look of peace on her face. I imagine it was hard, going back to that house, and if she needed to spend an hour crying, who can blame her?

God only knows what we'd have done if she'd faltered because, much as I loved Ruby, I'm not about to take on the world for her girls. If she can stand on her own two feet I'll stand by her, but I'm buggered if I'll carry her.

Georgie will be out of the house four days a week from now on, and Eliza for three, which is a load off my mind because having them here all day, every day, getting under my feet was driving me mad.

I can ignore Juliet, she creeps about like a little mouse and wouldn't dare to tell me what I ought to be doing. She's happy now she's back teaching, she's got three small boys coming for lessons each morning and then a couple more for the afternoons.

Emily, poor little soul, sits with them, as natural as you like and tries to do their lessons. You'd think she was the same age as them and truth to tell, since the accident, she is.

CHAPTER FOURTEEN

Eliza doggedly moved forward one day at a time, refusing to think of a future beyond tomorrow or view the past beyond yesterday.

The realisation that she'd have to support her sisters alone, terrifying though it was, drove her onwards and left room for little else.

Uncle Hugh was wonderfully understanding. He visited once a week for an hour or two and chatted comfortably about his own family and was sensitive about checking that the house was in good order and his nieces were as well as they could be.

After allowing a few months of mourning to pass he invited Eliza to join his family for a dinner once a month. 'I hope you'll accept. It will be beneficial for you to socialize a little and will allow you to renew your friendship with Alice. I'd like us to spend more time together.'

Eliza saw no way to refuse without causing offence. She was a solitary girl by preference, but she appreciated the security of having an extended family around her. She trusted Hugh and liked his family, particularly Alice. They'd been fast friends at school, each finding something they needed in the other.

Alice, having a handful of brothers, but no sisters, was thrilled to have a female friend and Eliza, excluded from the special union the twins shared, felt the same.

As they'd never entertained at home, Eliza was often stuck for words when meeting new people, which was awkward now she was the face of the library. She needed to push herself to be friendlier to strangers and this invitation might be the answer.

First though, there was an ugly scene to be dealt with when Georgie discovered she was not included in the invitation. She'd begun with tears and cajolery and ended up stamping her satin shod feet and howling.

Uncle Hugh would not be swayed. 'Eliza is the head of your family and an old friend of Alice.' He dropped a kiss on the top of her head which enraged her further.

Eliza hid her satisfaction. She felt some sympathy for Georgie but was pleased that Hugh didn't give in to her. Whenever they were together people only ever noticed her sister. If Georgie were to attend the dinner, she would be surrounded by a doting crowd in minutes and Eliza would be left on the fringes, looking like a fool and not knowing what to do about it.

The first dinner in St Johns was small. Just Hugh and his two younger sons, Nate and Gabe, with his daughter Alice as hostess. Eliza was the only guest and she was instantly at ease with her cousins, finding it easy to pick up where she'd left off upon leaving school.

The dinners grew larger and more formal as each month a new person was included. Gradually Eliza developed more confidence in social situations while building up a circle of friends and acquaintances.

Peter Andrews was one such. Having befriended one of the Daventor's - Eliza forgot which one - at university and being local, was invited to join them. He was smart and charming, not overly good looking, but with impeccable manners. He and Eliza got along well in a quiet way and he became a regular caller at the house in The Foregate.

Georgie alternated between hilarity that her sister had a suitor, and envy that she hadn't. She knew she was the more beautiful girl and she took care to always be attractive and ladylike, unlike Eliza who was careless.

Madame had once confided, a tone of longing in her voice, that she could make so much more of Eliza if only she could get her hands on her.

Georgie made a mental note to ensure that never happened. Being outshone by her bookish older sister could not be tolerated. She paid strict attention to Madame's words of wisdom. She had a lot to teach and, although working like this was fun, it was certainly not for ever.

If she had no money, and Eliza insisted this was the case, then she'd have to marry it, her aunt was in complete agreement.

Her passion for Freddy Daventor had begun when she was six years old and increased considerably when he went away to university. He was handsome and educated, and as he lived in London he must surely be more sophisticated than the people she ordinarily met.

They'd not met for years and he'd become godlike in her imagination. She was determined to make him fall in love with her the moment he came home from London, whatever she had to do.

In the unlikely event that he wasn't smitten at first sight she'd find someone of equal standing. Madame Eloise did nothing to disabuse her of her opinion that she was worth a Daventor, or better.

CHAPTER FIFTEEN

At the first scream Eliza was up and running. She grabbed a candle but didn't linger to light it. The darkness of the room held no threat to her, and she'd discovered that Emily was easier to calm in the half light.

She approached her sister's bed slowly, murmuring softly. 'Shush Emily, you're safe, I'm here with you, hush now.'

A silvery beam of moonlight illuminated the twisted face of the terrified girl, who thrashed about under the covers re-living the accident that had changed her life. She moaned and struggled to get free, drenched in perspiration.

Georgie - seeing that Eliza was there - quickly withdrew, heading for Eliza's warm bed.

The screaming eased at the sound of Eliza's gentle voice, and eventually ceased altogether, although the distressed girl continued to battle with unseen horrors. Eliza murmured on, her voice low and the words meaningless, but somehow reassuring.

Emily calmed, and Eliza lit the candle, but still made no move to touch her. She sat, watching and talking, keeping the soothing sound of her voice steady until the girl was ready to drift back to sleep. When at last Emily was still, and her breathing steady, Eliza moved forward to cover her with a soft blanket and stood by the door for a few seconds, breath held, hoping it was over. Some nights were easier than others.

These episodes, a nightly event in the months after the accident, had reduced in frequency and were now something to be dealt with once a month, for a night or two, and then were gone until the next month.

Experience had taught her how to calm Emily, experience had also taught her that although the twins would both sleep peacefully through what was left of the night, her own rest was over.

Emily's nightmares, distressing for the girl herself, and unsettling for her twin, were a constant reminder that Eliza had gained a heavy responsibility when she lost Ruby.

It was easy to indulge in self-pity after these events. The torment her sister went through was upsetting to see. Her own sleep had been disturbed and she'd be left feeling cold and afraid. Dogged by questions she had no answer for. How much longer would these episodes continue? Might it be forever? Who could help her? What chance did she have of finding a husband? Who would choose to live this way?

There was only one thing to do now Emily slept. Eliza shuffled into the kitchen and saw that Mary, as tuned into the month as she was, had left a jug of thick drinking chocolate warming on the embers for her.

She pulled her garden cloak around her shoulders and, jug in hand, stepped into the kitchen garden, which had been painstakingly restored after the storm and would soon provide much of what the family needed.

She strolled through this well-tended spot and out into the relative wilderness that was their orchard. There was no sign of the morning sun yet, but the sky was lightening up and she enjoyed the fresh bite in the air that would soon be whisked away along with the wreathes of mist that danced thinly above the stream and across the treetops.

She perched on a log and gratefully drank the warm brew, savouring every mouthful. When it was gone she jumped to her feet and completed a brisk circuit of their patch of land, needing to work off the tension she felt cramping her shoulders.

She loved the twins dearly, but she wished there was someone to care for her the way she had to care for them. Was that so wrong of her?

She spent her life explaining to everyone that the twins were inseparable and needed only one another and when things were going well that was true. When things went wrong however, she carried the burden of them both. Only she could settle Emily after a nightmare, and she took the full force of Georgie's tantrums.

Yes - she did bear a grudge and it was a battle to keep that nasty piece of self-awareness to herself. The thing she must do now was work off those bad feelings before they coloured the rest of her day.

She had time before her world awakened, and so she did a second, slower circuit, checking over the fruit trees and startling the pigeons.

It was she who had determined that the once neglected patch of ground at the back of their home should be utilised, knowing they had to be self-sufficient. She'd insisted they work together to plant the garden and ensure it was maintained. Seeing the trees laden with fruit gave her a feeling of proud satisfaction and her mood lifted.

She cast a vigilant eye over the fencing and what she saw gave her the first item on a list of jobs that should be attended to without delay.

It was a calm and in control Eliza Morgan who walked back through her door an hour later, ready to meet the day head on.

The kitchen had awakened and was now a hive of activity with Mary at the centre of it. She turned from the oven and scowled at the sight of Eliza.

Her damp hair hung down past her elbows like so many rat tails and the bottom six inches of her linen bed gown was caked and heavy with mud.

'Bad night again?'

'Asking the obvious again?' Eliza retorted.

Mary planted her hands on her hips. 'Don't you worry yourself about manners or my clean kitchen floor, Miss Morgan, I'll clear up the muck you're trailing behind you, you little madam.'

She tutted again as Eliza flipped a casual hand in acknowledgement.

Eliza hid her smile and thanked God for Mary. She had the sharpest tongue this side of the Severn, but she kept the wheels turning at home. She was a law unto herself, refusing to take direction and flat out ignoring most requests, yet she'd made it her mission to help Eliza through this phase in her life.

Since the night they'd cried together over losing Ruby they'd never exchanged a tender word, yet Eliza had no doubt that whatever trouble came her way Mary would be at her side.

CHAPTER SIXTEEN

MARY

The last kick up the arse I gave Eliza worked a treat.

It got the two of them out of the house for a few days a week and Juliet out of my hair, so I call that a job well done.

Mind you, even as I said my piece I knew how lucky I was to have got away with speaking to her like that. I couldn't have done it to Ruby and I won't be doing it with Eliza again. She's still kitten weak, but her claws grow stronger every day.

I know for a fact she'd been terrified of going back to that house, but she never uttered a word of fear or complaint, she just got on and did it. I reckon she impressed herself, and that's done wonders for her.

I don't expect any thanks, but I know I saved that girl.

She'd been forever in Ruby's shadow see, which I know pleased them both, but any half decent gardener will tell you that the strong plant will strangle or suck the life out of the weaker. It's nature.

She'll turn her mind to those papers she's been ignoring soon enough but I won't put the worry in her head. There's no sense in bringing trouble forward. It'll come soon enough, and she still needs time.

She took hell of a blow when Ruby died and if I hadn't stepped in Georgie would have got the upper hand. For all her delicate looks she's the stronger of the two. She doesn't feel the pain that Eliza does. Georgie's all about herself, while Eliza's all about the family.

If I'd have let them sit about fighting each other… well. I think Eliza will cope now.

Of course, she's getting no help from brainless Ellie whose encouraging Georgie in her nonsense. I know she is because since they've been spending all day every day together the girl has got that much worse. It's all I can do to not slap her sometimes. Flouncing around in a new gown and acting like a lady. It can't last.

I need to see Eliza growing in strength as fast as Georgie is because she'll have to handle her when it all goes wrong, as I know it will.

Thank God Eliza is Ruby's double because that soft Georgie is a pair for her idiotic aunt, and neither has an ounce of common sense.

CHAPTER SEVENTEEN

'I want to discuss our future.' Georgie announced one morning over breakfast.

Eliza looked up. The twins had dressed especially for this conversation and she was momentarily taken aback at the womanliness of them with their high bosoms and ridiculously small waists. They looked so lovely as they sat, smiling at her.

She felt a pang of sadness, they'd been identical, but as they matured the differences caused by the accident became more apparent.

Georgie shone, everything about her glowed with life and energy. Her hair, her skin, her eyes, her very nature. Emily was less somehow, still lovely, but lacking the vitality of her twin. She was slightly paler, slightly smaller, and so very quiet, usually content to nod happily at whatever Georgie said.

'Our future.' Eliza repeated. "Interesting, do explain.' She stretched her legs out under the table and leaned back, ready to listen, but on her guard.

Georgie usually entertained them at breakfast with an insultingly amusing story about someone she had attended to the previous day at Madame Eloise. Today's agenda sounded rehearsed.

'I think it's time we made more of an effort to meet people.' Georgie said as Emily nodded.

'What do you mean?'

'Weren't you listening, didn't you hear me?' Georgie demanded.

'My hearing is perfect, thank you. We're both out with people all day long and there's nothing I like more than to get home and away from them all in the evening, I thought you felt the same?'

Georgie placed her cup down very carefully and took a deep breath.

'Well, yes I did. But you see, I don't know where I shall meet my future husband. He's unlikely to stumble into Madame Eloise.'

Eliza relaxed, this was without doubt a scripted performance, so the least she could do was sit back and enjoy it.

'I think we should entertain here, nothing too grand naturally, but you know…we need to widen our circle. Try to meet new people. I do want to be married one day and I don't know how I'll meet anyone living as we do.'

Her lovely eyes brimmed with tears causing Eliza to sigh theatrically. 'You were doing so well, but the tears spoiled it. They work with Aunt Ellie because she hasn't realised you can produce them to order.'

Georgie sighed and then smiled prettily. 'Sorry.'

Eliza bit her lip. 'Has Aunt Ellie been whispering in your ear?'

Georgie's flush told her she scored a hit.

'I might have known, honestly Georgie of course I want you to meet men and have the chance to marry but what entertaining do you imagine we could do? Besides which, I thought you had your heart set on Freddy?'

Georgie cleared her throat, she and Aunt Ellie had given this a great deal of thought, fully aware that Eliza would be difficult, but both felt this was something worth fighting for.

'I've always dreamed about Freddy and when he's ready I do hope he'll fall in love with me.' She acknowledged Eliza's remark. 'But I think it's wise for me to develop a wider circle of friends as there are no guarantees in life. We should think about hosting a light supper with card games. It's important that we are seen in a social sense by our neighbours. I hear so much about girls in London who are to be launched into society and I so want to do something for me. Us!'

Emily's clapping hands were a meaningless distraction. Eliza realised this was a serious subject that wouldn't go away and wasted no time in sending the warning glances that Georgie had learned meant one thing. Stop now - we'll talk later.

That evening after Emily had gone to bed Eliza and Georgie shared a pot of Mary's hot chocolate and continued the conversation.

'Have you thought about what I said this morning?'

'I have. Before we get on to that I want to remind you to stop talking to Emily about … adult matters. I know it's hard, but you must understand that she really isn't the same age as you anymore. You do know that don't you?'

Georgie mangled her sewing around her hands and nodded sadly. 'I know it, but I forget sometimes. I can't explain.'

Eliza wrapped her arms around her. 'You don't need to explain to me, she's exactly like you, except you're growing up and she may not. The bond you share will always be there, but she won't always keep up with you. She tries to understand, but the grown-up world confuses and frustrates her.'

Georgie leaned into Eliza's shoulder and whispered. 'I miss her so much.'

Eliza stroked Georgie's lovely hair and blinked away her own tears. 'I know, I miss her too.'

They leant together and watched the fire flicker, both crying, but trying not to.

'It's almost bedtime.' Eliza eased her sister up gently. 'Tell me what you and Aunt Ellie are plotting because I won't do anything that might make us look foolish.'

Georgie pulled herself upright, sensing progress. 'But you wouldn't, because I've listened to the women I see at Madame Eloise and I know just what we must do. I've talked it all over with Ellie. We'd do all the work, we just need your approval.'

Eliza raised her eyebrows. 'We're not society ladies of leisure like your clients and I'm not going to pretend to be something I'm not. We'll look ridiculous and spend money we don't have.'

Georgie clasped Eliza's hands. 'I know that. Something small and simple here would be suitable. If you think about it, you'll see it's a good idea. How are people to know we're beautiful, civilised and available if we don't tell them?'

Eliza almost choked as she tried to keep the noise of her laughter down, nothing could stop the tears of laughter that filled her eyes.

'That was a direct Ellie quote, if ever I heard one. My God, *civilised and available*. You'd have done better to stay here with Juliet and learn how to be a governess, because listening to Ellie's nonsense will bring you nothing but disappointment.'

Georgie looked at her with pleading eyes.

'Georgie darling. I know you long for parties and a gay life, but that's not our world. I've never organised anything like that and I really don't feel I want to.'

'But you must see how unfair you're being. You go out to dinner with Uncle Hugh all the time and you have Peter calling in day after day, so everything is wonderful for you. But what about me? You call yourself the head of the family, so it's your responsibility to help me make the right match. I'm going to be an old maid, stuck here forever and I can't bear it.'

'Don't talk nonsense, you're far and away the prettiest girl in Worcester and very well you know it. I could name half a dozen young men who would offer for you tomorrow if you only gave them a chance.'

Georgie shuddered dramatically. 'Country boys, I'm not settling for one of them. I intend to make a good marriage and I haven't met anyone good enough yet. It would be so nice to be properly launched!'

Eliza muffled a snort. Poor Georgie read everything she could about society and the London marriage market and was desperately envious. She talked endlessly about girls in white dresses being twirled on the arms of dashing soldiers under the light of a thousand candles, all of which sounded like hell to Eliza.

'I wouldn't know where to begin Georgie.'

'I know and that's where I can help. When we're with clients they tell us everything. More than we want to know often!'

She pulled a shocked face and then giggled. 'But I listen when they talk about the dinners and balls they go to, and I've picked up some ideas.'

Eliza's look of horror had her backtracking quickly. 'No, not a ball, for us. But I do think we could do something very simple that would work well. And to be honest, a few more suitors would be good for you, Peter's not exactly…'

Eliza's look of offended outrage sent her running for her bed.

CHAPTER EIGHTEEN

Eliza resisted Georgie's entreaties, claiming the practicalities of opening their home socially to were beyond her. In truth she needed to know how serious Georgie was about the whole thing.

Georgie might imagine herself laughing and chatting with people she barely knew, but she was given to passions that were picked and dropped faster than she changed gowns.

This might be another such passion, and the fear of being left alone to entertain a group of people because Georgie was in a sulk had Eliza paralysed with fear.

Georgie held firm though, and after intense negotiation the sisters reached an agreement. Eliza would host a supper for a few friends and family – no music or dancing – and see how it went. She made it clear that Georgie was to greet everyone and remain in the room until the last guest left.

Eliza also insisted that Georgie agree to stay at home with Emily for one complete day, freeing Eliza to spend that day with Alice. This slowed negotiations because although Georgie longed for parties, she envied her developing friendship with Alice.

It took her a few days to respond with a demand of her own. 'I'll stay with Emily, but you must invite the Daventors to our parties, especially Freddy.'

Eliza looked at her sister in some surprise. 'But he's still in London. And even if he were here, don't you think it's time you grew out of your Freddy dream, you may not even like him if you meet him now.'

'He's rich and handsome and will fall in love with me the instant he sees me. That's what I've always wanted, and you know I have to get what I want.'

She waited for Eliza to look at her and then grinned cheekily, Eliza grinned back, Georgie could be fun when she wasn't being a brat.

Their first supper was confined to family. They played cards, and Georgie and Emily sang. Eliza managed to enjoy herself so much she decided she would try again the following month.

Their second supper exceeded Georgie's hopes when both Nate and Gabe Daventor joined them. In her mind they were practically society and their presence gave her a seal of approval. When they re-arranged the table seating so that they could flank her at supper, her happiness was complete.

She decided to petition Eliza for a couple of new gowns. Freddy must return soon and certainly he'd visit them, now his brothers had elevated them from family, to friends. And when he came, she would be ready.

Georgie was her brightest and best self at breakfast. 'Nate's friend seemed very taken with you last night.' She twittered. 'Peter was cast into the shade. If he doesn't pop the question soon he might find you swept from under his nose.'

Eliza blushed furiously. 'Oh, don't tease, Georgie. You know I'm not looking for a husband.'

'Oh, but you must be.' Georgie exclaimed. 'You can't pretend you're not, now you have two men interested in you. There's poor Peter, dull, but boringly reliable. And then there's your dashing new friend, terribly handsome and surely not nearly boring.

'I do think it's rather unfair that you have the admirers when it was my idea to socialize, but I'll catch you up, being younger and prettier.'

Mary's barely disguised snort as she bustled about with dishes was ignored by both girls.

'It might help if you made more of an effort though.' Georgie continued. 'You could aim higher than Peter, but it would take some work.'

Eliza spluttered. 'So rude Georgie!'

Georgie shook her head. 'No. Speaking the truth may be painful for the listener, but it's not rude. You don't dress any better at our suppers than you do to go to the library, and that's a dreadful mistake. I don't want you to settle for Peter, or at least, not until you've met a few more suitable men. I think it's wonderful that two men are taken with you and I hope you'll soon meet one that you like enough to encourage because it would be a shocking thing if I were to marry before you.'

Eliza sighed heavily and pushed her chair back from the table.

'I've no intention of encouraging anyone. Russell is the name of my new friend. He was thoroughly charming and not in any way boring. He spoke at great length about his fiancé and his forthcoming marriage. And why on earth which one of us marries first is of any concern to anyone else is beyond me.

'Those ridiculous creatures you and Ellie pander to have given you some very strange ideas and if I'm forced to listen to you carrying on like this every morning then I'll put a stop to our entertaining. The whole thing is meant to be a pleasant diversion, if you start acting as though it's some sort of a competition it will become miserable very quickly. I tell you Georgie, I don't very much like who you're becoming.'

Her fist landed on the table so hard the china rattled, after which silence fell.

Mary beat a hasty retreat, leaving Eliza and Georgie to consider each other in silence.

Eliza followed Mary out, but headed to her room in some confusion. Georgie's words had hurt her badly.

Should she want to fall in love and be married. Was she unnatural, odd in some way? What on earth was she supposed to do about it? She couldn't sparkle and flirt as Georgie did. Wouldn't want to, in fact. Holding a position as the centre of attention seemed like such hard work!

She left the house earlier than usual and wondered if perhaps Georgie had a point, maybe she should encourage Peter, make more of an effort to do whatever it was she should be doing. Although she really didn't think either of them had any interest in that sort of thing.

He was a constant polite presence, and yet they were rarely alone together. She didn't love him, but he was comfortable to be with. They'd shared a few personal conversations.

She'd confessed she'd be loath to relinquish her library work if her circumstances changed. He'd met Emily and understood that she'd always have a home with Eliza.

In return he had said that his widowed mother ran his home and would remain there. He didn't hint at a shared future and she didn't push.

She felt nothing of the love that Georgie, inspired by Ellie, talked about endlessly and longed for so dearly, but she'd grown to trust and depend on him. Family and friends were used to seeing them together, and Eliza had stopped protesting when Aunt Ellie smiled knowingly.

Life was certainly more comfortable with a handsome man available to escort her into dinner and to share minor household concerns with. She was content with the gentle pace of their relationship, it fit perfectly with her life and, wonder of wonders, had stopped Aunt Ellie pressing her to meet potential husbands.

There was a niggle of uncertainty in her mind though, she wanted someone who would care for her, cherish her even, she could admit that to herself. But when she tried to conjure up an image of who might fill that role, Peter's face did not spring to mind.

She'd witnessed with horror the passions that directed Georgie's mood and had no desire for that uncomfortable condition.

The girl constantly lurched from the heights of joy to the depths of despair. She suffered agonies if the one she hoped to see didn't notice her and was almost offended if someone she deemed unworthy dared to pay her any attention.

That nonsense was not for Eliza. Calm and considered was her way. Nothing to startle the horses, as Mary would say.

CHAPTER NINETEEN

Freddy Daventor strode along Threadneedle Street and through the magnificent archway that led to the Royal Exchange. He inhaled deeply and then sighed with pleasure, the very air smelled sweeter, he was sure of it. He'd been smitten since the day, five years ago, that he and Sam first visited.

What a revelation it had been. They'd both been as green as could be, foolishly imagining they were as sophisticated as any man.

Freddy had been unable to disguise his naïve excitement when he first entered this courtyard. The majesty of the buildings enthralled him, before he'd even seen the variety of goods that were for sale within the salons.

He'd stumbled along open mouthed, his gaucherie exposed. He itched to become a part of this lively and exciting world, so unlike anything he'd ever experienced.

They realise their clothes were all wrong and they struggled to understand the voices they heard ringing out. They made a pact to return only when they could fit in.

Five years on, he was as comfortable here as anywhere else and could stroll about nonchalantly, although he'd never quite mastered the air of boredom that Sam had perfected.

The racket from the market situated in the inner courtyard was no longer a shock to his senses. The teeming mass of humanity, conducting their daily business and yelling out insults and compliments at the same time, added to the character of the place and highlighted the air of luxurious restraint that could be found among the upper floor galleries that soared above their heads.

The buildings that bordered the courtyard were connected by covered balconies and this elevated promenade was the destination of choice for the smart set and was precisely where Freddy was heading.

From these heights the market scene below became pure entertainment. One could sit and drink or dine in comfort as the world passed by. Up here was where the most exclusive merchants and skilled craftsmen could be consulted.

Dress and manners were crucial and the clothing he wore cost more than he'd ever confess to his father and he'd cut out his tongue before admitting to his brothers how self-conscious he been the first time he'd walked about in such fashionable attire.

The Royal Exchange was where he wanted to be, and this was how one was expected to dress. His jacket, a rich dark blue was the perfect foil for his fair hair and clear blue eyes.

His tailor had advised him to keep the embellishments to a minimum and he'd listened and learned. His tailor was a wise man and nowadays he took his advice on all aspects of his dress. His necktie gleamed whitely and a small diamond, almost hidden within its folds, winked subtly as the sun caught it.

Freddy was blissfully unaware of the many admiring female glances sent his way. The women he met here were lovely, stylish and charming but…he didn't find any of them distracting enough to spend more than an evening or so with. He'd confided once to Sam that he found them boring and Sam had roared with laughter and slapped him on the back.

'That's the point of them, ornaments only. They want a husband and nothing more. Find a bored married woman for fun, they're always grateful and wonderfully discreet.'

Once he got used to the idea Freddy found the system worked very well indeed although he was tiring of it now. The society matrons were tolerant of a man sewing wild oats, but their sole aim was to see their daughters married and his reluctance was becoming a talking point.

He straightened his jacket as he reached the top of the stairway, his hand passing over the pocket that contained the message from his father. Sam was an unpredictable chap at the best of times and there was no telling how he'd take this news.

Until this morning the thought of Pa getting a sight of his tailor's bills had been the worst thing Freddy could imagine, but Pa had gone further than he'd dreamed he would. It wasn't all bad news from his point of view, although he'd never admit that to Sam.

All he wanted now was tell him and have it done with.

'Freddy, over here!'

Think of the devil and he'd appear, Freddy smiled and raised his hand. At least he wouldn't have to worry about Sam's reaction for much longer.

Sam indicated the direction he wanted them to take and Freddy nodded agreeably. He'd allowed Sam to take the lead in everything they did for years and rarely bothered to state his own preference, the few times he'd tried had caused ructions.

Today Sam was the very flower of fashion. Freddy could admire the superb fit of his green jacket, even as he winced at the vibrant shade. The extravagant gold filigree decorations on the front panels and across the cuffs were just about tolerable here, but heaven help him, he'd never get from one end of Broad Street to the other if he attempted to wear it - or anything like it - in Worcester. Sam had complete confidence in his own tailor and derided the restraint of Freddy's man.

He'd convinced himself that the Royal Exchange was fortunate to enjoy his patronage and he strode about in his finery, looking for all the world as though he'd been born here.

The two were cousins and had been friends since school. Sam was the ambitious son of a tradesman, determined to improve his lot in life.

He'd been a joke to the Daventors for some time. They laughed as he openly watched them, mimicking their speech and manners, and followed them like a lost puppy. Immune to their disdain.

Freddy, comfortable with his position in life, and bored by his brothers, began to encourage Sam's flatteringly devoted friendship.

Over the years Sam's drive overtook Freddy's indolence and Sam became the leader and Freddy the follower. He often wished he hadn't been so obliging, but, what choice had he had? Sam was an awkward cuss, it was easier to let things go, and the occasional glimpses of the insecure schoolboy he used to be made forgiveness easier.

'Oh lord, there's that crashing bore Martin. Quick, let's duck in here until he passes.' Sam muttered, bundling Freddy into a smoky chop house.'

Freddy shot him a knowing look. 'You've borrowed from him again? Christ Sam, you know what a leech he was before, why on earth did you go back to him?'

Sam waved a hand in the air. 'Nonsense, I simply don't want to get caught up with the fellow.'

Freddy wasn't convinced. 'How much?'

Sam tossed a careless grin his way. 'Relax. I've got his money and I'll repay him tomorrow. My allowance came through in the nick of time.' He raked his fingers through his dark curly hair. 'Life would be so much easier if Mama would loosen up, but she won't hear of it.'

He scowled, his lack of funds a constant thorn in his side. As the eldest son, he was the head of the family, and he strongly felt he should be managing their finances.

He was vocal in his opinion that she was a dull, provincial woman who had no idea how the world worked, yet her grasp on the purse strings was relentless.

Freddy's voice diverted him. 'If you have the money why not pay him back now, you know he'll add another day's interest on to the whole?'

Sam sneered. 'You sound like my sainted Mama and it really doesn't suit you Fred. Keep your womanish fussing to yourself. I'm attending a salon this evening and plan to double my money and then I shall be flush. Martin must wait.'

'You're a damn fool taking the risks you take.'

Sam walked out onto the balcony and Freddy followed, knowing the subject was closed. He shrugged, what Sam chose to do was no problem of his.

He leaned over the railing to gaze down on the heads of those lesser beings, forced to work under the bored gaze of those like himself, spending family money and killing time.

He watched with a half grin as a cheeky faced child approached a fat, slow moving gent and try to slip a tiny hand into his pocket without being noticed. A dog barked, the man turned, and the child was away, unnoticed.

Freddy turned back to the row of shops up here and drank in the sight. He'd miss it, no doubt.

Small card rooms stood alongside coffee shops, with milliners and dressmakers adjacent. Goldsmiths neighboured armourers while cobblers bordered gunsmiths. Birdcages could be bought along with mousetraps and fans. The walkways were already thronged with the most fashionable of London society.

This was where gossip was created, observed, and magnified.

Young women came to be admired by the men that had made an impression on them, if not their Mama's. Mature women came to be flirted with by men that were far more entertaining than their overweight, and decades older, husbands. Older men, with sufficient wealth, could be certain of a catch, if they cast their net's wide enough.

'Come on Fred, let's eat.'

He nodded cheerfully, this was as close to an apology as one could expect from Sam.

They strolled to Probert's chop house and were ushered to the central window seat, a compliment indeed, only the very best dressed clientele could be permitted to decorate valuable window space.

Sam grandly ordered the best the house could offer. Turtle soup followed by roasted beef served with cauliflower and onions. A sublime bottle of wine was quickly drained and two more were ordered.

CHAPTER TWENTY

Freddy removed the letter from his pocket and placed it on the table without comment, just sliding it towards his cousin.

'What's this, news from home?' Sam asked casually.

'Orders from home, I'm afraid. I'm to return to Worcester, Pa's had what he calls a 'concerning report' from Underhill and I've been left with no choice. I start for home next week.'

'Christ, I thought we could depend on another year here at least. What's his point? It's not as though he can't afford it.' Sam looked down at the letter with disgust.

Freddy nodded. 'I know, but there's nothing I can do, you know what he's like when his mind is made up.'

Sam flicked the letter between his fingers, a sneer on his face. 'It's your own bloody fault, you're so quick to criticize me but if you'd knuckled down you could have impressed the old bugger enough to get another year or two out of him.'

'God Sam, I'd no idea the law was as dreary as it is, there is not one aspect of it that interests me, and I can't hide my boredom. In truth, I feel a sense of relief knowing it's over. I hate the work and I hate old man Underhill.' He snorted. 'I don't know how you do it.'

'I do it because there's no family money swilling around to give me the choices you have, you lucky, lazy swine.'

Freddy laughed, but Sam's bitterness was real.

'So, you'll go trotting home and work for your Pa, is that the plan?'

Sam's voice was quiet, but Freddy recognised his tone and the white line around his lips.

'I'm sorry Sam, I know I've messed up our plans, but it's a miracle I've lasted as long as I have. I hate the idea of working for Pa, but what choice is there? The law is not for me.'

'But it's not just about you. We had an agreement. A shared office, working together. Are you going to crawl home with your tail between your legs and drop twenty years of friendship?'

'Not a bit of it. This is a stumble, nothing more. I'll go home, sweeten the old man…'

'Shut up and let me have a minute to think, will you.' Sam interrupted. 'You fall at the first fence every damn time. I'm not letting it all go, friends stick together. Remember.'

Freddy held his arm up to order wine for them. What choice did he have? Pa said jump, he had to jump. These past five years in London had been incredible and if it was time to go home, so be it. He poured a glass and leaned back, ignoring his brooding cousin. Nothing was ever good enough for poor old Sam.

He spent a happy hour, smiling at the pretty girls and sipping good wine. It was a beautiful day and if his time was almost up he'd enjoy every single moment here.

Sam reached out for the bottle, emptied the dregs into his glass and nodded. 'Hmm, let me tell you what I think we should do.' Sam swung out both his arms, as though to encompass all they could see. 'Worcester would benefit from a place like this, don't you think?'

'Oh Lord yes.' Freddy laughed. The wine was buzzing through his brain and he felt delicious softness wash through him, thankful Sam had taken his news so well.

'If for no other reason than to prevent u looking complete fools walking about Worcester dressed like this.' He stroked his lapel. 'This jacket cost so much, I don't see how I can justify not wearing it. I didn't realise how firmly stuck in the past home was, until we came here.'

Sam nodded. 'But here's the thing, there's nothing to stop us taking the fashionable world back. Worcester's prosperous, people have money and I'll wager they'd come up to speed pretty quickly if we showed them the way.'

Freddy shook his head, somewhat confused. 'I don't follow you?'

'If you're not for the law, maybe business would suit you? You should turn your mind towards opening something like this at home.'

Freddy laughed. 'The Royal Exchange, in Worcester, how could I possibly...?'

'Smaller, but every bit as select. You would need to start from scratch of course, finding a suitable building and negotiating with the right merchants, if you put your mind to it, you could pull it off.' He saw Freddy was not convinced but pressed ahead.

'We could still be partners, as we always said. Forget how impossible it seems. Put that out of your head and just imagine this being dropped into Worcester as it is. Can you not imagine it being thronged every day?'

'No. Honestly, I don't want a row with you, but you're either drunk, or you're dreaming. Worcester can't compare with London in any way.' He tried a diversion. 'I thought you were set on the law?'

'I'm set on earning money independently of my Ma. Knowledge of the law could be the first useful step into a business partnership. Come on Fred, for God's sake wake up! Something changes, and you just sit back and let it happen Why don't you liven up and think what your next step might be?

'You've buggered this up and I would think you'd seize upon any chance to build a business that works the way you want it to. Your Pa's made it clear that he's not going to be funding your studies and longer. I think I have a solution that will work for us all if you'd only open your mind.'

Freddy put his hands out palms together, and then opened them, as one would a book. 'Fair enough, tell me what you're thinking.'

'I'll continue with law and we'll open an office as we agreed. I'll practice law and you'll take us into business. We always said we'd work together and this would work in our favour. No outsiders involved, you watch my back and I watch yours.'

Freddy drained another glass and raised no objection. 'Sounds better than working for Pa. I'll give you that.'

'You won't have to do that, if you'd only trust me. I'll start looking into legalities and such, you go home and start behaving like a good son, we'll need Hugh on our side.'

'Why?'

'I want you to get your hands on our old school.'

Freddy opened his mouth to protest, but Sam was ready.

'Hear me out. It never took off properly and if it hadn't been for the dozen blasted cousins it would never have even started. What a ridiculous idea, building a new one on the doorstep of the Kings school.

The place has been abandoned for years and someone should get in there before it falls into rack and ruin. Why not us? You'll inherit it one day after all. I'm suggesting we take it over now and show Hugh how to make some real money.'

Freddy choked down his laughter. 'Now I know you're drunk. It would never be mine, Arthur is the heir.'

Sam shook his head in temper. 'I know he's the heir and I know you're a disappointment to your Pa.'

'Steady on.'

'You know it's true, Arthur's the golden one, but Arthur's never going to be a business man. You need to convince your Pa that by giving you the building, he'll be helping you start your own little empire. He understands that world and he'll give you a chance if he sees you're sincere.'

Freddy swallowed deeply, here was the expected anger and now he felt obliged to diffuse it. He forced a laugh and clapped Sam on the shoulder.

'You accused me of fussing like your Mama an hour ago and now you've turned into my Pa, what on earth has happened to us Sam, have we gone mad?'

Sam wiped his hands over his eyes and then grinned. 'Not yet we haven't. Come on, let's go and have some fun and put work to rest for the day.'

They walked out into the cool air and Sam grinned. 'Look over there, Thomson and his sister. You know, the pretty one who simpers when she sees you. Come on, let's try to find them. One last fling before we head home, eh?'

They ambled around the balcony in harmony.

Freddy was relieved that he'd told Sam the law was not for him.

Sam was satisfied he had planted a seed for the future.

CHAPTER TWENTY-ONE

Before the day had properly awoken Eliza was up and eager to start her day with Alice. She slammed the door and set out, feeling lighter and brighter with every step she took.

It was all she could do to not break into a run. They rarely did anything of any importance together and yet this one day a month shone like a beacon.

A whole day away from Emily's nerves and Georgie's tantrums was a joyous thing. She could be frivolous, admit her fears, and not be judged weak. She could giggle and be silly, listen to gossip, and discover who she really was.

Georgie insisted that she was selfish for refusing to share this day with her, but Eliza would not relent. It was the freedom of this day that gave her the strength she needed to deal with the rest of life.

Despite her rush to see Alice she slowed her pace outside the store front of Pargeters. She didn't want to be caught by Aunt Ellie, because that would mean thirty minutes lost forever, but she wanted to check her reflection in the biggest, shiniest windows in the city.

Everyone who cared about their appearance stopped here and, since spending time with Alice and being lectured by Georgie, Eliza found that she was starting to care a great deal more.

She gave a half turn, pleased to see that the simple green gown she wore suited her form perfectly. The colour set-off her reddish-brown hair, the curls of which gleamed in the morning sunlight, her green eyes sparkled, and her cheeks were healthily pink. After tidying away a stray curl she tilted her head saucily and smiled at her reflection, liking what she saw.

Eliza followed the Morgan side of the family, sturdy and strong, and with a quick brain that pleased her more than beauty would have done. She was blessed with a gift that lovely Georgie might never have. Eliza liked herself and envied no-one.

She strode out briskly, looking out for Alice as she neared the cathedral grounds and, on seeing her cousin ran forwards, Alice did the same and they were quickly wrapped together in a hug of genuine warmth.

Alice pulled back and looked at Eliza. 'You look wonderful, better every time I see you.'

Eliza smiled happily. 'I'm happy, the library is good for me and home has settled down. Georgie is on a mission to build up a few admirers and it's wickedly entertaining to see how easily she has young men dancing to her tune. She's shockingly cold about the whole business and persists in her childhood plans to marry Freddy eventually, of course.'

Alice pulled a comical face. 'She's going to be horribly let down you know. My brother is charming, but terribly lazy, and unbearably vain. He wouldn't be the object of her dreams if she knew him half as well as I do. Underneath his gloss, he's as dull and ordinary as all men. More on him later!'

She linked her arms with Eliza as they walked and swapped family news. The conversation soon swung back to Georgie and her selfishness.

'Hmm, if Freddy is all you say he is, they might be well suited. She's so entranced by her own beauty she can't walk past a mirror without pausing to study herself.

And she's the laziest cat in three counties. We should pair them up without delay, they deserve one another.'

Alice laughed. 'Just desserts, and all that... I'll come along to one of your suppers one day, for the pleasure of seeing her cutting the youth of Worcester down to size. It's difficult though, Pa would worry about me getting across the river safely after dark and yes - I know I could stay overnight with you, and I would love to do that – but there's always so much work to do at home. But I will come soon, I swear.'

They followed their usual route towards the market hall where there was always plenty to see.

'Let's see what's new in Worcester this month.'

Together they made a striking pair, an equal match in height, but differing in almost every other way. Alice was a curvy giggler with a youthful voluptuousness that she had only recently learned to enjoy. Her hair was a tumble of golden curls that shone with health and her eyes were a clear light blue, both features clearly marked her out as a Daventor.

Alice had the kind of looks that attracted the attention of men wherever she went, but she took none of them seriously. She'd managed her father's household for years, taking care of him and her five brothers single-handedly. Men and their foolishness held neither delight nor surprise for her.

As the two young women linked arms and leaned in to each other they became oblivious of their surroundings until they passed Oswald's Coffee Shop and Eliza inhaled the heady aroma of coffee and tobacco.

'Wouldn't you love to step inside and see how they react?' Eliza felt irritation each time she passed a place that denied her entry solely because she was female, and yet welcomed any man, no matter how disreputable.

Alice screwed up her face in disgust. 'No, truly the whole place will be rotten with old men dribbling and young men farting. You romanticise these things too much, we're much better off without them you know.'

Eliza choked with laughter at Alice's vehement dismissal of the mystique of men, but Alice barely paused for breath.

'Now come on, Pa's promised me a new gown and we're going to choose the fabric today.'

Despite their wealth Uncle Hugh hated showiness and was considered 'careful' with his money.

'If he's splashing out on a new gown there must be something afoot. What's the occasion?'

'Well, I said earlier that there would be more later, and this is it.'

Alice took a breath. 'Pa wants to throw a dinner, rather more grand than normal to welcome home my returning brothers. He intends to re-introduce them to local people and hopefully launch their careers.' Alice hooted with laughter. 'You'll be invited, naturally.'

Eliza smiled broadly. 'Brothers, plural?'

Alice nodded and squeezed Eliza's arm in excitement. 'Yes. You'd better prepare Georgie for this, Freddy will be home from London within days, permanently! He wanted to remain in London, but Pa says he's spent enough on his education and he's ordered him to come home and start working. He and Sam are still as thick as thieves and there was talk of them starting up as lawyers in Worcester, but Pa sets no store by that. He's stomping about in a fury and I've barely managed to convince him to let Freddy get home and tell us what he plans to do. Pa's about ready to horsewhip him without hearing a word. You know what he's like.'

Eliza wafted her hand in front of her face and slumped into a mock faint. 'Oh lord, there'll be no holding the girl.' She laughed. 'But I can't imagine uncle Hugh taking a horsewhip to anyone.'

'No, he's usually a sweetheart. But he's bitterly disappointed that Freddy hasn't applied himself. But when did he ever? There was letter from the chambers that drove him so wild with anger I heard him cursing about it with someone. Pa says he's wasted the past five years and he won't let him waste any more.'

Eliza thought it wiser to not comment. Alice was free to criticize her own brother, but she might not take kindly to her cousin doing the same thing.

'The news that just might save Freddy's skin is that Arthur's been offered a place at the Infirmary in Worcester. He did terribly well at Edinburgh and could pretty much choose what to do next. Pa's bursting with pride.'

'I should think so, that's a marvellous thing.' Eliza said, remembering the quiet studious boy from school. Arthur hadn't run with the pack, preferring his own company, and happily relinquished the position of leader of the dozen cousins to younger brother Freddy, who was far more suited to the role.

In fact, Eliza was the only one he'd ever had any time for, they'd shared some classes and were a match for one another in many subjects. When he'd been in danger of getting too stuffy or pompous it was only she that could tease him out of it.

She smiled with genuine pleasure. 'I haven't seen either of them for years. It will be good to have them home.'

'Oh, it will.' Alice agreed. 'I've missed them both and Pa will be easier in his mind having them nearby. He's sad that neither has any desire to join him in the business though, so I can see some battles ahead. Arthur is unlikely to change his direction, and as for Freddy, he's going to have to do as Pa tells him and he won't like that.'

Eliza had mixed emotions regarding Freddy, he'd always been wild, frighteningly daring, a rule breaker who saw fun in every situation. He never studied, yet absorbed knowledge easily, tests and exams were a breeze for him and he wasted little time on those not so blessed. She guessed they'd all changed since then.

The girls embarked on a morning filled with laughter and teasing as they consulted dressmakers, milliners and a shoemaker. Eliza quickly became caught up in Alice's spending frenzy, deciding she also needed a new gown.

They were both tired and almost delirious with the thrill of spending too much money when they eventually sank onto their seats in the discreet tea room opposite the Guild Hall where they habitually had lunch on their day out. This was the time they most enjoyed, swapping confidences and sharing dreams.

They watched as a young couple strolled past, holding hands gazing adoringly at one another.

'She's going to be forcibly kissed before this day is over if she's lucky.' Alice said matter-of-factly.

Eliza's eyes sparkled. 'What do you know about being forcibly kissed?' She demanded.

Alice straightened her shoulders and tried to look prim. 'I read a great many novels, as you well know.'

Their laughter drew the offended attention of a matron who grasped her avidly watching daughter by the arm and rapidly marshalled her out of earshot, causing them to erupt once more.

As the outraged mother stepped in to the street Eliza's eyes followed her only to see an older woman, standing some way back, her eyes fixed on them. She didn't look away, even when she was spotted. Eliza frowned.

Alice touched her arm. 'What is it?'

Eliza shook her head and mustered a smile. 'Nothing, I thought I saw someone I recognised.'

She turned her attention back to her friend. 'How dull it must be, to live in a constant state of righteousness. I'd much rather laugh in a vulgar manner when something amuses me.' She grinned wickedly at Alice.

Alice looked around to make sure she was not likely to be overheard before leaning forward. 'I can't imagine what the old witch would think of this though. I should have said that until last week my experience of being forcefully kissed came from the pages of novels...'

Eliza was transfixed, all thoughts of prissy matrons gone. 'Last week? What? Who?' She grabbed Alice's hand and demanded information.

Alice leaned in closer. 'His name is James, he's the nephew of Mr Daniel, you know the tooth man in St Johns?'

Eliza shook her head impatiently, but Alice carried on regardless.

'Oh, you do. Anyway, he's apprenticed to Mr Daniel, so he'll be in St Johns for years. He's tall, though not as tall as Arthur, and he's very thin. He doesn't eat enough, I'm sure of that. He has the blackest hair and grey eyes. His face is serious, but when he smiles my heart pounds and when he's near me I can't look anywhere else. I dream of him making love to me.'

Eliza's eyes gleamed. 'He makes your heart pound and inspires you to talk to me of love, yet this is the first I hear of him. Explain yourself young lady!'

They edged closer to one another, heads touching. 'He arrived two months ago but no-one saw him as he was closeted with his uncle, learning about his new situation, I imagine.

'They joined us for supper two weeks ago and I tried not to be obvious, but my eyes kept going back to him and each time, he was looking at me. He looks deep and serious but when he smiles, well...'

'But the forcible kissing? Give me details, please.'

Alice squeezed Eliza's hand in excitement. 'I took him for a stroll around the grounds after supper last night. Just to the river and back.'

Eliza squeezed back. 'And he kissed you. Forcibly?'

'I'm not sure.'

'Alice, how can you not be sure? Stop teasing me.'

'I think I may have kissed him.'

Their giggles made speech impossible, and when the sour faced waitress bustled over to straighten their table in a vain attempt to quell them, they were lost.

Her withering scowl only made them laugh harder.

Alice wiped her eyes. 'Pa would be furious if he saw me making such a scene, but I'm so happy.'

'Tell me all.'

Alice reached over the table to fiddle with the dismal looking plant that sat there, dying for water, and Eliza saw her hand was shaking a little.

'We walked and talked, he's clever and witty, and interested in me. As we turned to the house, he leaned towards me, to offer his elbow and I couldn't help myself, I kissed his cheek. I could hardly breathe, but he smiled and held my hand as we walked. He's promised to call on me for tea tomorrow.'

Alice had no foolish fancies about men, she knew and understood them, and Eliza realised this was an important development. 'I must meet this man, you can't be having ardent lovemaking with a man I don't know.'

'You shall meet him. I sense something wonderful is about to happen and I feel thrilled knowing that when it does I won't resist. I feel that in every fibre of my being and nothing that could possibly happen will change that.'

Eliza swallowed the lump that had appeared in her throat. Glowing cheeks and sparkling eyes had transformed her cousin from pretty to beautiful.

She felt a selfish chill, was Alice slipping away from her so soon?

CHAPTER TWENTY-TWO

Eliza grasped the slimy hand rail of the ferry that would take her to St Johns, an unpleasant but crucial precaution. The boards she stood on were slick with mud and moss and it was all she could do to remain upright as the going was rough.

She braced herself as they reached the mid-point of the river where the currents were most treacherous, today however they sailed through and she relaxed as they approached the far shore with no upset.

She straightened the hem of her new gown, an extravagance, but quite glorious. Once she felt secure, her gaze flitted over the other passengers and were met by the sharp eyes of Caroline Wenderby, peering over her fan and rudely drinking in every detail of Eliza's outfit.

At once she wished she'd used the bridge to cross the Severn. It was a hard walk from The Foregate to the Daventor house and she'd have arrived uncomfortably hot but might have avoided prying eyes.

Not that she had any secrets, it was the feeling of being constantly observed then being forced to explain her movements that infuriated her. Eliza tried desperately to not mind but she always felt that she was being judged and she'd never mastered Ruby's knack of not giving a damn.

Every stitch of her clothing would be reported back to Caro's old friend Aunt Ellie in detail before nightfall tomorrow as would her ultimate destination. Aunt Ellie would come calling to fuss about her foolishness in leaving home and travelling about alone, but with every intention of discovering who else had attended the dinner and to sigh sadly that she had not been on the guest list.

Eliza shrugged then smiled. Uncle Hugh would send a carriage to meet her on the other side of the river and imagining the envy that would rouse in Caro's mean and jealous breast was sweet but fleeting.

Georgie would hear about the carriage from Ellie and that would ignite another storm of anger and jealousy not unlike the one they'd had earlier. Despite having an abundance of admirers and an adoring crowd gathering in her home once a month to pay homage Georgie always felt she was never quite getting her due.

'Why am I not invited? I don't understand.' She had screeched earlier.

Eliza patted her hand. 'It's a private family supper, I'm going as Alice's special friend, to save her from spending the whole evening waiting on a room full of men and having no fun herself.

'Our cousins are home for good now and I promise we shall have them here to visit us just as soon as possible, and there will countless opportunities for us all to get together throughout the summer.'

Georgie pouted. 'Well, it's unfair and I wish you would tell Uncle Hugh so. He must be made to understand that I am not a child and should not be excluded.'

'And yet here you are, behaving like a petulant ten-year old.' Eliza snapped as she felt her spirits drop. 'Go away and let me finish dressing.' The door slammed hard enough to cause Eliza to wince and grasp for the vase that was sent flying in the draught.

Georgie had chosen her moment well, having been mid-way through dressing Eliza's hair. All she could do with the disastrous tangle was brush it out and scrape it back in her usual style. Fanciness didn't suit her anyway, she reassured herself.

The ferry bumped into the bank, jolting her out of her daydreams, and she hastily gathered her cloak around her and picked up the bag that contained her evening slippers. As she was handed up into the waiting carriage she turned and smiled a goodbye to still watching Caro.

CHAPTER TWENTY-THREE

Hugh had done his best to mark the return of his sons appropriately, given their differing circumstances.

He was deeply proud of Arthur who'd successfully completed medical training and had a wonderful career ahead of him. He'd have liked to throw a grand affair to celebrate his return, but Arthur hated social engagements and would have disliked a bigger event.

Freddy, who loved nothing more than a grand affair, and was at his best when surrounded by a crowd, was only home now because he'd been ordered back because he'd idled away the past five years.

A modest dinner with a few carefully selected friends and neighbours struck a comfortable balance.

Eliza dutifully went to rescue Arthur who'd placed himself on a couch and was staring morosely at the huge painting of a hunting scene that had hung above the fireplace for so long that there couldn't have been a brush stroke on it that was unfamiliar to him. He jumped visibly when she spoke.

'How wonderful it must feel to be back at home with your family, after all this time.'

He eased his collar and looked distracted. 'It is of course, but after eight years of solid studying and meaningful work, I find this kind of thing…' He shrugged, '…frivolous, to be honest with you. What are they chattering about? They see one another several times a week and yet they go on and on about the same old thing endlessly. I don't know why they bother.'

'They're here to welcome you home. They do see each other often and it's more than likely they might prefer to be doing something other than sit here tonight, but they're showing friendship and respect to you and Uncle Hugh, and it would be a courtesy if you could make the effort to do the same.'

Arthur's mouth clapped shut, but not before she saw his thin lips twitch. He turned to face her and clasped her hand.

'Cousin Eliza, you haven't changed a bit and you're absolutely correct, I'm acting like a bore.' He leaned close and whispered. 'It's easier to let Freddy shine, but I know I mustn't be lazy.'

At that they heard a laugh coming from the corner of the room. Freddy, not feeling the pressure of his disgrace in any noticeable way, stood at the centre of a group of people, all of them smiling and listening to what he had to say.

He turned and caught her eye, raising his glass in a silent salute. She lifted her hand to wave, then dropped it to her lap, feeling foolish.

She turned to Arthur. 'Let's circulate together, I'll remind you of their names and you can smile and be polite for an hour. How does that sound?'

The following hour demonstrated that while Arthur had gained confidence and knowledge he'd lost all sense of humour. Whatever the topic of conversation, he was right and one who disagreed was wrong.

She looked up once saw Freddy watching her, his face a picture of pained pity for her plight. She turned her back, trying desperately not to laugh.

Arthur was a man on a mission, committed to righting the wrongs of society. He had no time for the pleasures in life and no patience with those that did and didn't hesitate to make that clear.

It was with relief that, after an hour of wheeling him around and ensuring that he exchanged a few words with everyone, Eliza considered familial duty done. She led him back to the couch and his scrutiny of the painting.

She saw Freddy approaching and relaxed.

'We must meet soon, I want to talk to you without that shocking bore Arthur hanging about. My dear cousin, you've done sterling work this evening forcing him to be civilised, and you shall be rewarded. Did you ever meet such a pompous ass? Do you suppose everyone leaves medical school with all joy stripped from their soul or were we simply unlucky with my brother?'

She fought to contain a burst of laughter. 'Don't Freddy, he's not that bad.'

He picked up her hand and kissed it. 'You sweet girl, he's that bad and worse. Steer clear of him if you want to keep that lovely smile.'

He nodded a farewell as he was claimed by another friend who couldn't wait to welcome him home.

She envied the way he made everyone in the room feel special, his permanent smile and quick wit made him the perfect dinner guest.

She scanned the room, looking for Alice. Her duty was done and now it was time to be introduced to the famous James. If Alice was falling headlong in love it was up to her best friend to be sure she landed safely.

He seemed to be a pleasant young man, but perfectly ordinary to Eliza's mind. She was not in the least disappointed when he was whisked away by his uncle, allowing her to sneak outside with Alice to sit on the wall looking up at the stars, as they had years ago.

'He's very handsome.' She said, without being asked.

'He is, isn't he?' Alice beamed in recognition of Eliza's good taste. 'And he's called on us three times now, so we know that he's serious. Do you like him?'

'Will it change anything if I don't?'

Alice looked behind to be sure they were not overheard. 'I hope you do because yesterday he definitely kissed me and now I'm totally ruined. You have to give your approval!'

'Hmm, were you abandoned?'

'Almost.'

They rocked with laughter. Alice was in love and Eliza was happy for her.

'What are you two cooking up?' Arthur's voice from behind made them pull apart guiltily before Alice grinned and beckoned him to hunker down and squeeze in between them.

Alice explained. 'I was about to tell Eliza that you need somewhere to stay in Worcester.'

He put a brotherly arm around her and nodded to Eliza.

'Hmm, I've been offered a room at the infirmary but there's not a moment of peace and quiet there and I'll have to continue studying so I'll need a place to escape to. I'd prefer to stay here, but it's just too far away to be practical. I'll be on call at all hours once I start and I'd never get out if I had to come all this way.'

Duty and manners overrode her reticence. 'But you must move in with us.' She said. 'We have an entire floor unoccupied. You could have a bedroom, a study room and a room to sit and be comfortable in, and all your meals found. You'll have company if you wish, all female I'm afraid, but you can escape up to the third floor for peace when you need that. And we're only a walk away from the infirmary.'

Alice nodded happily. 'I felt sure you'd say that, it's the perfect solution isn't it Arthur?'

He squeezed Eliza's shoulder. 'I should be grateful, if you're sure you can cope? It would make my working life so much easier and Pa will be happy to know I'm with family. He's worried about where I might end up.'

'As if we would consider you staying anywhere else.' Eliza declared stoutly.

He wasn't the Arthur of old, but she could work on him, and besides, having a doctor at home might be useful in view of Emily's situation. Not to mention Georgie, surely having him as a house guest would improve her manners.

CHAPTER TWENTY-FOUR

MARY

Just when I think she's got everything under control Eliza invites one of those blasted Daventors to move in. I'll make a good show of it, but I won't forget how badly the old man treated Ruby, wicked bastard he was.

Having his kin in my house turns my stomach, but I'm only the bloody cook and bottle washer, so my opinion counts for nothing.

And the work it took, she wanted the three rooms on the top floor - unused for years – emptied, scrubbed and polished, and then re-furnished. The whole house was upside down for a week. You'd have thought the bleeding king was coming to stay.

Then she reminds me that he'll need to be fed at all hours. A trainee doctor works when he's needed I was told, and so could I make sure there would always be something ready for him?

Bleeding cheek. I expect I'll be the one washing his clothes as well!

She did offer to get a girl in to help me with the heavy work but I'm not having some snit in my kitchen getting under my feet and stealing our food. Looking after the Morgan girls is my job and I'll bloody well do it.

Georgie's skipping all over the place. A Daventor is as near to royalty as she'll ever get and if she can't get one brother, I daresay she'll settle for the other. It's not my place to tell her she'll never be more than their poor relation.

Eliza was there, scrubbing and polishing and doing the dirty work while Georgie and Emily pulled apart madam's wardrobe, deciding what she ought to wear if she was to impress him.

I heard her telling Eliza she'd need a couple of new gowns to wear in the evenings when Arthur came home. Made me laugh when she suggested Eliza might want to smarten herself up too.

Eliza wasn't bothered though. She told her bluntly, 'Arthur will be helping with our bills in exchange for lodging here. There will be no candlelight dinners or new gowns.'

Georgie did her best. 'Aunt Ellie says our cousins could be helpful to us in the future and we should nurture them.'

Eliza, who had been polishing an old cabinet of Ruby's, threw her cleaning cloth at Georgie. 'I'm nurturing no-one, but if you want to impress him I suggest you knuckle down and help me prepare his rooms.'

When he did eventually turn up he was dead on his feet and as scruffy as you like. My heart went out to him to be honest. He was a walking ghost, white faced and shabby to the point of being dirty. Not the lordly fellow I was expecting not Miss Georgie, going by the shock on her face as me and Eliza half carried him up to bed.

I had to strip off his filthy clothes before I could let him lie down because I didn't want the infirmary stink on my clean linen and I can tell you, he's no more than skin and bone when he's naked.

I left him there and he slept for six solid hours.

CHAPTER TWENTY-FIVE

Eliza handed the bundle of morning post over to Georgie having discovered that allowing her to open their latest invitations and pass comment gave her so much pleasure that she was usually the picture of good humour over breakfast.

'Oh, a picnic on a river boat, lovely, we'll accept that I think.' She hummed as she flicked on through the envelopes. 'Mrs Simkins and her daughters are having a tea - I'll make sure we're doing something else that day – too dull. And this one is to you, not us!' She tossed a flimsy letter back to Eliza.

As Georgie read the next glossy invitation Eliza used a knife to open her own letter. She scanned it and hastily slipped it into her pocket for later digestion, having no wish to share the contents.

She had a full day at the library planned, although the first hour would be spent with Ana, which was always a joy and could never be considered work.

Together they chattered away about anything and everything and yet Eliza didn't want to share the letter with her either.

What with the business of the day, and the entertaining the family in the evening it was past midnight before she was alone and could face the letter, and consequences, without onlookers.

She sat in a chair by the open window of her bedroom and let the words sink in.

My dearest Eliza,

I have pondered long and hard and have concluded, sadly, that our wonderful friendship must remain just that. Our circumstances make anything else impossible.

Your sister needs to remain in familiar surroundings and I understand your reluctance to leave her.

I cannot uproot my Mama and I will not abandon her. It would be impractical financially for me to keep two homes.

My dear, I see no future for us and can only ask you to remain a trusted friend to me as I will to you.

In that vein I hope you will listen to some advice from a friend. I urge you to reconsider your situation, and Emily's needs. There are nursing homes that can offer a level of care that cannot be met at home. My dear, why not let her go and thus find freedom for yourself?

I shall spend the summer in Europe and will be announcing my marriage upon my return.

Your friend, Peter.

Eliza had kept a hold of her emotions all day, firstly by imagining the derision that she'd have been subjected to from Georgie at breakfast if she'd had one sniff that Eliza had let her only suitor slip away, but now she could give free rein she was surprised to feel bitterly angry, but not in the least bit tearful.

Peter didn't matter to her as greatly as he might have imagined. Her strongest emotion was one of fury that he would let her down so thoughtlessly, almost casually. She was surprised, having assumed they were both enjoying their gentle relationship.

Looking back, she realised how much information she'd given away and yet how little she knew about him. Clearly, he hadn't been interested in her, he simply wanted to know what she had that he could convert into assets before he made her an offer.

It stung to know he considered her unworthy of marriage, although she should probably thank her lucky stars. Her primary emotion was anger, damn the cowardly man for making her look a fool in front of the world.

Nothing would prevent Aunt Ellie from telling her where she'd gone wrong. And then would begin the awful business of parading a succession of suitable men for her approval. Well, she'd take that because she had no choice, but she would not be laughed at.

She glanced at the letter sitting on her lap and then tore it to shreds, the beastly man had spoiled her day. And the unkindness of him, he'd be away in Europe for six months and on his return would be announcing his forthcoming marriage. To whom? Did he keep a string of spinsters around as a failsafe? Had he found one with more money, or fewer sisters?

She lay down in the dark and spent the greater part of the night pondering the letter, determined to be settled in her own mind before she aired her change of circumstance and was forced to listen to the opinions and advice of others.

Peter was clearly less of a gentleman than she was a lady and there was comfort in that. The ending of their relationship would raise few eyebrows and she'd struggle to hang on to her pride.

They'd accepted invitations on the strength of him being her escort so naturally people would wonder. She'd have to find a way to convince people that she'd not been let down.

Alice would back her. She'd have to say that Peter, realising he cared more than she, had given her back her freedom - like the gentleman that he was.

She grimaced at the taste of those ghastly words, but she'd rehearse with Alice until she could say it with conviction.

CHAPTER TWENTY-SIX

Eliza and Alice shared a customary hug and then Eliza bit her lip and took a deep breath. 'I need your help.'

Alice smiled prettily. 'Anything.'

'Peter has released me from our arrangement.' Eliza said flatly.

'Oh, my goodness, this calls for sustenance.' Alice declared, pushing her into the nearest tea room.

They sat down in a small booth at the rear and Alice took her hand. 'He's cut and run? What a pig!'

Eliza nodded, and Alice looked at her searchingly. 'I have to say you're managing to conceal your utter heartbreak incredibly well.' She put her head on one side and waited for more.

Eliza shrugged. 'I'm angry, and surprised. It wasn't a love match and there was nothing formal agreed between us, but I had thought...'

She absently stirred her tea with a cake fork and looked out into the distance. 'I do think he's behaved shabbily, but I'm not terribly sad. I want you to help me put a good face on it though, I can't bear to be left looking like a fool. Will you help me?'

She pointed her fork at Alice, who smiled grimly. 'I most certainly will. I hope you gave him a piece of your mind and didn't let him slip off the hook too easily?'

'I haven't seen him, he wrote. He's in Europe and informs me that on his return he'll be announcing his engagement.'

Alice was outraged. 'He sent you a letter! He's not just a pig, he's cowardly and unkind and he must be a liar! People should know about his shoddy actions.'

'No, because I will not be left looking like the girl he left when he found someone better. I need you to support me in that.'

'He'll have been depending on that won't he? He's going to get away with acting like an absolute swine because we want to protect you. What sneaky, low way to behave.'

Alice tightened her lips. 'And our story is that he's released you from your agreement?'

'Because he knew my heart wasn't engaged.' Eliza recited.

Alice snorted. 'You've been reading those ghastly novels I told you about!'

A serving girl approached them only to be briskly waved away.

Eliza continued. 'What I'll be saying is that Peter and I were good friends and had never been more than that. He's gone off to Europe with my blessing and good wishes.

'Naturally our families know there was more to it than that, but there was nothing official and no-one outside of family will be rude enough to question me, will they?'

Alice shook her head with a confidence she didn't entirely feel. 'No.'

'He was also kind enough to advise me that putting Emily in a home would increase my chances of marriage.'

Alice gasped and put her hand to her chest.

'Oh, he didn't put it as brutally as that…clinics…better care…freedom for me and la, la, la. He's sure no-one will take me on with her by my side.'

Alice reached across and held Eliza's hand. 'But you know…'

'No Alice! Not today.'

'No, of course.'

It was Eliza that broke the silence. 'He'll be away for six months which leaves me time to say what I need and to let the dust settle.' She sighed heavily. 'Aunt Ellie will no doubt cry, that's how she copes. Uncle Hugh will rage and talk of horse whipping and then it will all be forgotten. I want everyone to know I'm perfectly happy and I wish him well. Peter remains a dear friend.'

Alice nodded thankfully. 'Well of course you can rely on me but what a beast he turned out to be. How do you really feel?'

'I'm so angry I could scream.' Eliza burst out when the serving girl, who was trying to listen to what was going on, had gone.

'But I'm relieved too. I've had a lucky escape, imagine how terrible it would be if I'd loved him?' She gurgled with laughter. 'I couldn't bear to be pitied though, so will you help me?'

'Need you ask, really?'

'It's partly my own fault, I could have been much more encouraging towards him, but I chose...well...I don't know. What do I want? I could have made it happen and I didn't, why?'

Alice refreshed their tea cups and replaced the pot on its stand.

'Possibly because he's as dull as ditch water and you'd have been settling for less than you are worth. He should have swept you up and made you forget everything but him, that's what you deserve. You should be glowing with expectation after being kissed, lips bruised and breathless. But we both knew he was never man enough to take control.'

Alice smiled before biting into a pastry and then grinning wickedly as she licked her lips. 'This has more substance than Peter, and it's so much sweeter.'

Eliza laughed. 'True.'

'I want you to find a man who makes you feel the way I do now, with James. This absolute joy and certainty that whatever happens, he'll be by my side. Peter never could have made you feel the way I do.'

Eliza kissed Alice on the cheek. 'Let's not speak of Peter again today, not now we have a James to share. Be careful though Alice, abandonment has its consequences.'

Alice dimpled prettily. 'I'm a country girl, with five brothers. I know how nature works and I won't come to harm through ignorance. Besides, he's a good man from a good family. I'm safe and so very happy. Now, what say we go and buy matching hats?'

They tried on hats, posing this way and that, they pinned on brooches and draped shawls around their shoulders, parading up and down the aisles in stores the length of the High Street. Both more interested in each other than the goods on display.

Alice gripped Eliza and pulled her forward for a kiss. 'Do you ever wish we could do this every day?'

'No. This is fun because it's rare. I enjoy hearing about the differences between us. You live your life, over there in St Johns taking care of your Pa and your brothers, thinking that men are all fools - all bar one – and completely at sea without a woman ushering them forward.

'I'm in my house with the girls and Mary, envying the freedoms that men have. Seeing you once a month is a perfect luxury for me and I don't want it to change.'

'And we're so good for each other.'

'We are.'

CHAPTER TWENTY-SEVEN

Eliza and Ana huddled together in the window seat of the library and watched the deluge that had descended on Worcester with such speed that the main London road had become a small river.

Ana wriggled out of her damp cloak and made herself comfortable. 'I'd sooner sit here and talk to you than go out in this. What else is happening at home, are you coping with your cousin?'

'To be honest, I don't see much of him which suits me. He's a self-important bore. I knew he had no sense of humour, but I had hoped he'd be a decent conversationalist but if it's not medicine, he's not interested. One word of politics and he glazes over.'

'Aye, well politics does that to me.' Ana laughed and patted Eliza's knee.

'Yes. But you have other interests and you've taught me a great deal. But him, well I think he should be more aware of the world, he's benefitted from the best education money can buy and all the advantages that go with that, and I don't think it's good enough for him to ignore the world now he's got what he wants.'

'Bless your innocent heart, that's men all over.'

Eliza carried on as though she hadn't been interrupted. 'He keeps harping on about Peter Andrews and what a fool I must have been to have ever entertained him. He called him a useless dandy.'

Ana grinned widely. 'Not quite as strong as my words but…'

Eliza nodded. 'But I don't see why I should be made to feel foolish by Arthur who knows nothing about anything. I'm very disappointed in him.'

Prior to renewing their friendship she'd fondly imagined that a person wanting to work in medicine might be driven by the desire to help other people and it had shocked her to realize that the patients Arthur cared for were not so much people, as a set of intriguing symptoms only he had the intelligence to understand.

Since having him in her home, she realised the wisdom of Alice who insisted that men were not clever or mysterious people, but rather ineffective muddlers.

If an evening with Arthur was any indication of what an evening with a husband was like, Peter had done her the greatest favour ever.

'He sits in silence and when I look up he's watching me. It's uncomfortable.'

Ana frowned. 'Does he frighten you?'

'No, not in that way. But he looks at me as though I'm odd and he certainly thinks I lack brains. He'll chirp on about the food we eat and the dust he sees in the house. It's as though he thinks he can improve me, which of course makes me want to aggravate him more. He asks why I insist on working, then throw extravagant suppers. He makes me want to scream. We work because we should, and our suppers are as plain and simple as can be.'

'You don't have to explain yourself to him.' Ana interjected.

'Georgie spilled crumbs over the table, she was thrilled to receive a particular invitation, you know how excitable she can be. He clicked his tongue at her, as though she were a badly-behaved child. And yet he was sitting there with his scruffy hair and wearing a dusty jacket. He thinks he's perfect and no-one else is quite good enough.'

'So, he's not going to be a match for either of you.'

Eliza scowled. 'Perish the thought. Mercifully he works such long hours that I can forget about him for days on end.'

Ana stood up and stretched her back. 'You might be making a mistake there. Ignoring him, I mean. It's not easy, but when someone offends you, they should be told. I'm not saying have an argument with him, but you should tell him not to talk to you that way. How else is he going to learn that you don't like it?'

'I couldn't.'

'Why? Because he's your cousin, or because he's a man? If Emily or Georgie said those things to you, or sat about at the table like he does, would you speak out?'

'Well, yes, of course I would.'

'Then why not to him? He's sharing your home and he should treat you with respect. If he fails, then remind him.'

Eliza thought about that. There was no doubt he wouldn't behave the way he did if Ruby was still here. She'd have told him directly what she thought of his manners and his dress.

'How does Georgie handle him?' Ana asked.

'She's pathetic, she blushes and smiles on demand for him. Aunt Ellie's influence I'm afraid, she thinks a woman's role is to gain approval from men. Quite the wrong thing to do in my opinion.'

'You need to manage him. Letting him get under your skin is as useless as blushing. Show some spirit.'

Eliza nodded. 'Enough of this. Tell me what you would have been doing had the rain not trapped you in here?'

By the time the sun came out they were both laughing as Ana told her about a fight she'd witnessed the previous evening.

'I can't say which was the wife and which the girlfriend, but the more they slapped at each other the more scared the poor sap looked. I'll bet his gallivanting days are over!'

CHAPTER TWENTY-EIGHT

Eliza took a stub of candle and patrolled the silent house.

On the first landing she heard a deep rumble and snort followed unmistakably by a long fart. Mary was settled for the night.

Moving on she pressed her ear to the heavy dark set of double doors from behind which came the burble of her sisters as they prepared for bed.

The room she'd adopted as her own was little more than a corner that had been carved out of their larger space, but she managed to slip in without attracting their attention.

Heavy curtains divided the two spaces and she pulled these closely together before flinging open her windows, welcoming the bite of breeze that licked her overheated and pounding brow.

She rarely gave a thought to her future, there was always so much to do in the here and now, but things were changing all around her and she was very much afraid of being left behind.

Georgie had a string of admirers and would be married and off in no time, she was lovely, she was witty, and she was ready.

It was an open secret that Alice was dreaming of marriage and children. Since falling for James, she could talk of little else and even Hugh had begun to tease her about how sorely she'd be missed and how badly they'd all manage without her once she set up her own home.

Tucked away in the half-light, Eliza acknowledged her envy. She didn't have their freedom and never would. She had to – wanted to - take care of Emily. There wouldn't be room for anything else.

Falling in love was not for Eliza. Peter had made it plain no-one would marry a girl with the obligations she had, and she'd never abandon Emily, so that was that. She'd make a sensible and calm choice or accept being left alone, dull and matronly, safe, but unsatisfied.

The library had been a life saver, her desire to keep it going and her willingness to go back into that building had stood her in good stead. She was proud of herself for doing what she had but now the novelty had worn off, she found it beyond dull, though she'd never admit it to her family.

Ana knew. In fact, Ana knew pretty much all there was to know about Eliza and was quick to jump in and offer advice when asked. Her guidance was less conventional than that offered by Alice, and refreshingly tempting.

Alice opined that, if she bided her time, a suitable husband would appear, and all her troubles would be over. Ana declared that sitting about waiting for a husband to gallop in and solve everything was the sign of a weak mind. She expected better of Eliza.

Eliza thought the same way as Ana, it was time she found something to make her life more satisfying, but what, and where should she look? Should she even be looking, was it selfish to want more from her life? What wouldn't she give to sit and talk to Ruby one more time?

She tossed and turned all night and consequently slept late. She rushed in for breakfast, nodded a good morning toward Georgie and kissed Emily on the top of her head as she poured herself a cup of chocolate. She rifled impatiently through the post, her mind still on herself. Would she ever again put herself first or was she destined to be the old maid looking after others? Why couldn't she be young and silly and wasteful and free?

'Aunt Ellie thinks you and Arthur would make a good match.' Georgie trilled, nudging Emily and watching Eliza's face.

Eliza coughed into her hot chocolate and whirled around in fury. 'Georgie, I swear if you repeat that within Arthur's hearing I'll never forgive you.'

Georgie shrugged carelessly. 'Well, it could suit very well. He knows us and all about us. He needs a wife and you're not as young as you were. How mortifying will it be for you if I get married first? I can't be expected to wait for you to catch up if I have an offer you know. As head of the family, I would imagine you'll see that things happen in the right order.'

'And with those few spiteful words you're spoiled my day. I swear I don't know how you can bear to look at yourself.' Eliza threw her cloak over her shoulders and stepped out into the morning air, slamming the front door so hard the knocker reverberated.

She had yet another cause to bitterly regret encouraging Georgie to work with Aunt Ellie. They brought out the idiocy in each other and their flights of fancy often reached ridiculous heights, but this was beyond bearing.

And how dreadful if Arthur started to think that way, a refusal would be mortifying for them all. She heartily wished she'd never invited him to share their home. It had never crossed her mind that might view her as a potential wife.

And she'd have to turn him down because to be married to him would be would be a fate worse than death. She'd have to increase her efforts to avoid him and she must be sure to never, ever be alone with him again.

CHAPTER TWENTY-NINE

'Eliza, I'd very much like a moment of your time, if you can spare it.' Arthur's words sent a shiver down her spine, made worse by Georgie's smirk. He'd been trying to isolate her for weeks and she'd been as devious as she could, taking every effort to avoid being alone with him and only relaxing when he was out at work.

This direct a request couldn't be ignored. She carefully avoided making eye contact with Georgie whose eyebrows seemed to have developed a life of their own.

'It's my day with Alice so we can walk together if you're ready to go now.' A spiteful move as she had two hours before meeting Alice, but if he wanted her he could at least forego breakfast.

She resigned herself to letting him say what he had to say and then she'd settle the matter. It would hurt Uncle Hugh, but there was nothing else for it. Arthur was dull and pompous and not even for Uncle Hugh would she consider him.

He was forced to gulp down the piece of toast he'd bitten into and look with regret at the coffee he'd just poured but must now abandon. Even so he put on his coat and together they headed into The Foregate.

They walked in silence, he seemed to be searching for words, so she occupied herself running through the list of things she wanted to accomplish that day. They got as far as the Cross and still he hadn't spoken. 'I'm going this way.' She said, pointing.

He reached for her hand. 'I must speak to you. It won't take long' He pointed to the newly opened tea room. 'Let's go in there.'

'Of course.' She allowed him to clasp her elbow and guide her towards the narrow doorway.

He pushed open the door and froze as a bell that was attached to the door alerted everyone in the room to the arrival of a newcomer. A half-dozen matrons turned to inspect him, and she saw the back of his neck redden. He stood, mouth agape, then half turned, as though to make a bolt for freedom but a serving woman blocked his exit.

Eliza took pity on him and stepped forward to lead him through the over furnished room, meeting all interested gazes with a cool smile.

'Do women like this sort of thing?' He asked, once they were seated.

She shrugged. 'Not me, but I can't speak for all of them.'

He looked taken aback at her remark but gathered his wits enough to order tea and then waited, fingers drumming on the table until they were served. He politely thanked the woman who delivered their tea, despite his crushing disappointment when he saw the two rather sad slices of an unidentifiable cake that came with it.

Eliza took pity on him. 'In their defence, places like this are a haven for girls like Georgie who need a safe place in which to meet friends and chatter. I'm more inclined to go for a walk alongside the river and keep my own counsel'

He nodded and struggled to swallow a lump of the cake.

'I often wonder what the frills and fuss might be covering, though.' Her pity had evaporated.

Arthur dropped the piece of cake he'd been about to devour and looked around anxiously, presumably for signs of vermin.

Teasing him was no fun. 'Really Arthur, you must try to relax more, you're always so…tired. We see little of you at home, do you never take time away from your work?'

He rubbed his hands across his face and mustered a smile. 'There's always something to be done. I try to allocate a day a week for tasks outside of the infirmary, but the demands are such that...'

Eliza poured their tea as he recited, with tedious detail, the pressures piled upon the shoulders of a young doctor. When his voice tailed off she filled the gap with chit chat about the twins, all the time aware of Arthur looking at her speculatively until she couldn't bear it the strain any longer.

'Arthur, won't you please tell me what's troubling you.'

He looked shamefaced. 'I'm sorry, I know my manner irritates you and I apologise, I do try to be…accommodating, but I've failed. I do see that. I've encountered a situation that I think you must be unaware of and I'm afraid I can't ignore it, but I'm also afraid that bringing it to your attention will anger you.'

Her dark mood lightened and drifted away. If he was afraid of her anger, then perhaps a proposal was not imminent.

'Go on.'

'It's about the mother and baby home.'

She waited for him to continue.

'They're being starved of funds, so much so that people in need are being turned away if they are unable to pay. Surely that flies against everything that it was originally opened for?'

She looked at him in complete confusion. 'Why are you telling me?'

He looked at her as though she was an idiot. 'Because it's your responsibility, you're the owner.'

'I must be particularly dull today. I honestly have no idea what you mean.'

He infuriated her then by reaching out and tapping the back of her hand in reproach. 'Do you pay no attention to your affairs?'

She shook of his hand. 'I manage the library, and we get a small income from…'

Arthur tutted. 'I suggest you start paying more attention to your own business and spend a little less time reading the newspaper in the evenings. I can't imagine what has been going on with no-one taking charge. Don't you receive regular reports from your agent?'

She responded automatically to his question. 'I'm sent a quarterly statement of course. I've never asked for more.'

'And yet you're spending money like water. Georgie had a new gown just last week, though the butcher hasn't been paid. You can't drift from day to day, living hand to mouth.' He sighed dramatically, and with a great deal of satisfaction.

'Your livelihood rests on your investments and it's your responsibility to ensure that they are being managed correctly. You must want to know more about where your money comes from and how long it will last? I'm sure you'll marry one day, but until then you can't sit about not knowing what you're worth until...'

She put her hand up, silencing him. 'I've left everything to the agent because everything was in place for me to do so. You're quite correct though, I should be better informed about my position. I've never questioned the arrangements, but you can be certain I'll rectify that.'

He nodded his approval. 'I do hope you will Eliza. I'd hate to think of wrong being done in your name, you were always the cleverest of my cousins and I'd like to think that the good work that Ruby did will continue through you.'

She resented his patronising tone although his comment about her being the clever one went some way toward saving him. 'I've said I'll investigate and I shall.'

He coughed importantly and looked around, presumably for eavesdroppers, although no-one in there paid him any mind. 'I'm hearing some worrying stories about profiteering, that's what's prompted my concern. The home has been a refuge for a great many women over the years, it will be a tragedy if it's allowed to fail.'

Eliza flushed with temper. She hoped her neglect hadn't damaged anything of Ruby's, but if he kept on speaking to her like she was a badly trained dog she'd slap him.

'I'll do what I must. Thank you for bringing this to my attention.'

'Yes, of course.' He spoke stiffly, his hurt at her tone clear.

She unbent. 'Really, I do thank you Arthur. I'm grateful to you for pointing this out. But you do labour a point once you have one.'

She reached up and kissed his cheek before turning to walk away her mind racing. Hugh had handed her a pile of paperwork, when Ruby died, and she hadn't looked at them since.

Self-pitying fool that she was, she should have been learning about what mattered and not whining that she missed her. It was time to put that right and dig into her business.

She had a problem to solve which was lovely, and no unwanted proposal to fend off, which was even lovelier.

CHAPTER THIRTY

'I think I should go and see the trustees and talk to them and I was hoping you might come with me.'

Alice had the look of a trapped rabbit. 'I couldn't, Pa would never forgive me.'

Eliza looked at her in surprise. 'But, you do see I have to do something.'

Alice was unconvinced. 'You probably need a more reliable agent, but you really can't go dashing off to their offices alone. They won't talk business to a woman anyhow. Pa will be furious that Arthur has mentioned this to you.'

Eliza looked at Alice with disappointment. 'I felt sure you'd want to help me. This is my business we're talking about, and if things are not being managed correctly, surely I have the right to demand an explanation?'

Alice continued to shake her head. 'Yes, through an agent. I understand that you're concerned about what you've heard, and I know you're having to be very careful with money so why don't you ask Pa to go and talk to the agent on your behalf?'

Eliza shook her head in frustration, Alice had such fixed ideas about what was right and wrong, and she'd become even more rigid since the wonderful James had become her closest confidante.

'Alice, I can't ask Uncle Hugh, he's got far too much to worry about, and I don't know any other men. Well, Arthur of course, but he's never got a moment to call his own. I'm sure if we went together and presented a united front I could make my point.'

Alice pursed her lips. 'Absolutely not. You've always been obsessed about what men can do that women can't, and I've never agreed with you. You're asking me to do something I'm completely against. You don't know how things work, how could you possibly expect to make a difference? All you'll do is make a laughing stock of yourself and if you feel you must I can't stop you, but I won't let you do to the same to me.'

They looked at each other, both a little shocked at her vehemence.

They dropped the subject, neither of them wanted to argue so there was no clearing of the air. They talked a little of James and a little more of family matters, but neither enjoyed the rest of the day.

They were both sadly relieved when they parted.

CHAPTER THIRTY-ONE

'Well I don't know why you're wasting time talking to all and sundry about it. If you're short of funds, get down there and kick up a fuss and stay there until you put a stop to it.'

Ana's advice was more to Eliza's taste. 'I know, but Alice thinks it's not respectable.'

'And it's probably not, but how much longer are you going to let that silly little twit prevent you from doing what's right?'

Eliza giggled uncomfortably. She loved Alice and felt disloyal talking about her with Ana, but Ana was so refreshing and always straight to the issue, seeing no sense in 'going around the houses' as she put it.

'You keep taking advice from the likes of her and you'll lose your spark my girl. It's time to make up your own mind and do what you think is right. You've got Alice telling you to be a lady, Georgie telling you to be a marriage broker and Mary ordering you about from sun up to sun down.'

Ana plonked herself back down in her seat. 'Now listen to me, Alice is a nice girl who's been brought up in a house full of protective men, men who've dictated every moment in her life whilst making sure she was kept busy in the kitchen cooking for them. It's all she knows so we can't blame her for it. But you're not Alice, and there's no family of men ready to pick you up when you fall.'

Eliza recognised the truth of those words.

'You were brought up in a different way and now you're alone. Decide for yourself, if it goes wrong you've learnt something. If it goes well, you'll trust yourself more next time. I know it's frightening but you can't lean on anyone but yourself.

'Consider the voice of Miss Alice against our Ruby. Which one has done the most for you? Which one do you most admire? And which one do you think you take after?'

'I know. But I'm…'

'You're waiting for somebody to tell you what to do and Alice just did. That's the problem with letting others tell you what to do. You end up doing what they want you to do, not what you should. It's tough, but you're on your own. If you believe there's something wrong you've got a duty to get to the bottom of it yourself. You should be down there knocking on their door right now!'

CHAPTER THIRTY-TWO

Eliza pushed open the wooden door to the entrance of Givens, Givens, and Givens, and found herself in a waiting room far more luxuriously comfortable than her home.

The rug she stood on was richly patterned and the heavy mahogany furniture that lined the walls was buffed to a rich glow. Several lamps were lit, and a small fire glowed a warm welcome. The silver candlesticks glittered, unlike the tarnished ones at home. She walked slowly around the room, picking up the small objects that all served to suggest a grand room in a country house.

A door opposite the one through which she'd entered opened and a clerk stepped forward. He quite openly scanned her from head to toe, his eyes finally stopping on the porcelain plate she hastily replaced.

He sniffed and crossed to the table, where he adjusted the position of the plate before turning to her 'Good morning Madam?'

She swallowed her nerves. 'I'd like a word with Mr Givens, if that is possible?'

His smile was a formality that failed to warm his eyes. 'The nature of your business? We do have three of them.' He coughed out a stuffy laugh after reciting what was clearly his favourite joke.

Eliza, embarrassed at being caught snooping, was sharp with the pompous man. 'I'm Eliza Morgan, I need to speak to whichever Mr Givens manages my holdings.'

She moved towards the fireplace and slowly removed her gloves. 'I'll wait.'

The clerk nodded and backed out.

She heard a door open somewhere in the back of the building, the clerk's voice was muffled, as was the reply. A door slammed, footsteps drew near, and the clerk came back into the waiting room, his smile a little warmer.

'Miss Morgan, Mr Givens senior is the man you want. He's not free today but can call on you at your home on Tuesday if that is convenient? It might be helpful if you could tell me what specifically you wish to discuss?'

She thought for a moment. 'Tuesday will be convenient. Please inform Mr Givens that I'd like a full report on my business.'

She felt energised as she stepped out into the fresh air. Mr Givens had probably been there, but reluctant to see her for some reason and she realised that was a good thing. She had a few days now to learn all she could and would be forearmed for their appointment.

She should talk to Mary, she had to know something about Ruby's business dealings. And it was time she went through the boxes of paperwork that were lying unopened.

She had been blithely ignoring things she was afraid of and if there was anything wrong she could blame no-one but herself. She'd work hard to make up for it though. She smiled at the thought and turned towards home only to see Aunt Ellie bearing down on her.

'What brings you away from the library today?' She asked as she enveloped the younger woman in a lavender scented hug.

Eliza hugged her back warmly, Aunt Ellie was silly and a snob, but she was also kind and loving. They walked slowly side by side and once the family pleasantries were complete Eliza voiced her thoughts.

'Business. I've been drifting along in ignorance but now I've decided to educate myself. I've arranged for Mr Givens to give me a full report, it's time I shouldered some of my own responsibilities.'

Aunt Ellie's smile faltered. 'Well, you should know where your money is invested of course, but don't be hasty. You know nothing of business and nor should you. My advice is to leave well alone, business is for men who know how the world works. Your husband can worry about all of that for you, when you marry.'

Eliza merely smiled, and Ellie misunderstanding her silence touched her hand gently.

'You mustn't worry my dear, the man for you is out there you know. It's too soon for you to give up hope. Be patient.'

Eliza laughed and hugged her. 'Oh really, Aunt Ellie, I'm perfectly happy alone. And I don't know that I will want to make any changes, I just think I should know a little more about what is being done in my name. I'm quite sure Mr Givens will be happy to co-operate. I've been remiss, and I want to put that right. And who knows, I may even have an idea, or two, of my own.'

Aunt Ellie looked appalled. She gripped Eliza's hand, almost desperately. 'I'm not at all happy about that. I'm going to ask Sam to call on you. He's back from London and I'll feel easier in my mind if he can oversee things, despite his lack of experience. Now don't shake your head my dear, let me do this for you.'

Eliza accepted gracefully. Sam and she had never seen eye to eye as children, but that was years ago. He'd probably grown up into a stuffy man in the same way that Arthur had. If she was fortunate Sam might be as passionate about contracts, agreements and accounts as Arthur was about medicine. In any case, having him on her side couldn't hurt.

She kissed her aunt soundly and they walked their separate ways.

CHAPTER THIRTY-THREE

Eliza ignored the message from Sam that came later, advising her to delay her appointment as he'd be unable to attend.

Bolstered by Ana's encouragement she felt she didn't need Sam to hold her hand at this stage. She had questions she wanted the answers to and thought she would be wise to listen to what Mr Givens had to say. If she was unclear after that, she could turn to Sam and together they could decide what action to take.

Her confidence took its first knock on the day in question as she found herself faced with all three of the Mr Givens'.

Mary showed them into the parlour. 'Shall I stay, Miss Morgan?' She asked respectfully.

Eliza smiled grimly and nodded. Mary was never respectful and only ever addressed her as Miss Morgan when she was especially put out about something. She'd perceived the same threat that Eliza had.

Eliza indicated that the men should sit, and she was even more on her guard when all three took chairs side by side, facing her across the table. She opened her mouth to speak only to be interrupted by one of them. Eliza couldn't tell them apart.

He read out a stream of dry legal sentences and meaningless numbers and she made a valiant effort to hide her confusion as her brain struggled to sift the unfamiliar jargon that came at her in waves, he droned on and on and her head began to spin with the effort of keeping up.

She dug her nails into her palms and remembered what Ana had been telling her for the last week. She was in charge here, whether they realised it or not. She took a deep breath and stopped worrying about their words and settled for assessing the three men sitting on the other side of her dining table.

They reminded her of predatory birds. Their dark musty clothes and dry, dull expressions were designed to intimidate, she was sure. When one spoke the other two kept their beady eyes on her. She was heartily glad Mary was in the room with her.

'My dear Miss Morgan, your account is all quite straightforward and there's nothing for you to concern yourself with. If matters are to continue, all we require is your signature on these documents. Your affairs - I'm certain you'll agree - are being profitably managed and we see no reason to change anything.'

He slid the documents across the table toward her and raised his eyebrows impatiently. 'If you would just sign at the bottom there.'

Eliza reached her hand out toward the inkstand and then paused, before allowing her hand to drop onto the table. 'Forgive me Mr Givens, I'm quite with such matters. Explain to me again why it is that you need my signature now?'

Mr Givens senior cleared his throat and licked his lips and she smiled to herself. He was doing an excellent job of demonstrating how difficult she was being, and how patiently he was handling her.

Another Mr Givens embarked on an explanation. 'Miss Morgan.' A smile and a gentle sigh. 'Let me recap for you. Mrs Ruby Morgan, your aunt, left everything she owned to you.'

'Miss.' Eliza interrupted.

'I beg your pardon?'

'She was Miss Morgan, she never married. And in the name of accuracy – crucial, I'm certain you'll agree - we should note that she was my grandmother not my aunt.' Her gaze ran across them from left to right, but not one of them looked her in the eye. 'Pray, continue.'

He cleared his throat. 'You were sole beneficiary of Miss Morgan's estate. The entirety was placed in our hands to manage on your behalf. The business, and your income has been protected; guardians, administrators and lawyers were contracted, and everything continued as it had before…'

She nodded her head. 'And my question remains, why do you need my signature now? And why did you think the three of you needed to come and get it?' Each word was clearly enunciated and again she looked at their faces in turn as she spoke. She ignored Mary's snort, keeping her face straight and her eyes on the vultures.

Some unseen message passed between them and the younger one responded. 'It's a common business practice, Miss Morgan, and you couldn't be expected to know this, but when a person of property is planning for the future it's important to protect the interests of those who will inherit. You were a child at the time the will was written and could not have been held responsible for the management of the estate. You've now reached majority and so the contracts must be re-issued.'

'Or not.' She said flatly.

The snort from the corner of the room was less muffled this time and the men shifted and glanced uncertainly at each other before turning their eyes back to her.

Mr Givens senior decided to take the matter back in hand. 'We must have your signature if we are to keep your businesses functioning. If you don't sign, we can't act for you.'

'I understand that much. Allow me to tell you what I don't understand and what you are failing to explain. I called this meeting because I've heard troubling reports and I feel obliged to ensure that everything is running in exactly the way Ruby wanted. All you seem interested in is obtaining my signature. I find that alarming.'

Her eyes scanned the three faces. 'I came of age some time ago, yet you've made no effort to explain matters to me, offer me advice or indeed obtain my signature. I wonder, has there been an oversight in your office?'

She smiled sweetly. 'If so - and here you must forgive my ignorance - could there have been other oversights?

'Please stop wasting my time gentlemen. We'll leave the issue of my signature to one side until you explain why the mother and baby home is turning away desperate women with means?'

She took a deep breath. 'Then you can tell me why Sansome Springs Pleasure Gardens has fallen into a shocking state of disrepair?'

They looked at each other, glanced at the unsigned papers and then back at each other. The one in the middle raised his hands, as though surprised at her stupidity.

'Miss Morgan, we were appointed by Miss Morgan to manage her affairs – in the event of her untimely death – ensuring a secure future for you and your sisters, and we have done so. Your signature will enable us to continue.'

Eliza folded her arms. 'You have provided an income, that's true. However, you haven't answered my questions, and that does not bode well for our future.'

She stood and nodded to each man. 'I need time to consider matters. Leave these papers with me and after I've studied them I'll make my decision known to you.'

He spluttered and looked to his brothers for support. 'But Miss Morgan, we cannot act without your signature.'

She remained standing and smiled at him. 'Indeed, you cannot Mr Givens.'

She stood perfectly still until the three men made their exit and it was only when she heard the slam of the street door that she allowed herself to sink into a chair.

'Don't fret, you did the right thing. Bloodsuckers was just after more of your money. And you can always sign the blasted things tomorrow if you get a fit of the jitters.' Mary patted the top of her head as she made for the door.

'I'll be bringing up your tea in a few moments. You better get stuck into all that paperwork, you've got a fair bit to plough through.'

Eliza put her hands on the table to stop them shaking, she felt faintly sick, but also jubilant. She'd faced the three of them alone and they hadn't bullied her. She'd retained the upper hand it felt rather wonderful.

She immersed herself in the paperwork that lay before her.

CHAPTER THIRTY-FOUR

'Did you do anything about the matter I drew your attention to last month?' Arthur said, his head on the side as he waited for an answer.

She bit her tongue, wanting to ignore him, or tell him to mind his own business, as Ana advised. 'Yes. I've done a great deal.' She said.

'And?'

'And you're going to be late for the infirmary if you don't hurry.' She smiled sweetly and ignored his angry grunt.

'Very well.' He huffed, before precisely lining up his used knife and fork and nodding goodbye.

Georgie sniggered. 'He's not happy with you, is he? Didn't you fall at his feet when he proposed? I'd have refused him flat out, but I've got more choices than you. You shouldn't keep him hanging for too long though, he might go off the boil like Peter did. You'll get a name for yourself, cold and bookish. You're spending so much time reading those stupid reports that you're turning into a sloppy bumkin you know.'

Georgie ran from the room laughing, and Eliza thumped the table in frustration. The annoying girl managed to hit a sore spot every time she aimed, and it was becoming more of a battle to laugh off her more spiteful barbs. Sometimes she thought her sister really disliked her.

She listened as Georgie left the house and then a few moments later Juliet's students arrived for their daily lessons. Mary started rattling about in the hallway and at last she knew she could count on a few hours of peace and quiet.

She sat down to balance the household accounts and lost herself in receipts and bills. She was keeping on top of things but that was with three of them working. How had Ruby managed to support them all? She flicked back and forth through the ledger almost certain the answer didn't lie there. She closed the book in frustration seconds before the door knocker rattled.

'I'll get it.' She called out, knowing if she ignored the caller, Mary would respond, but then she'd be subjected to sly digs about ladies of leisure for as long as it took for the woman to get over it. It made for a happier home to do it herself.

The man who stood there looked familiar. He was tall and dark, he had an easy smile and his hair curled and shone with health. He carried a silver topped cane in one hand and a glossy hat in the other. He inclined his head before speaking. 'Eliza?'

She didn't instantly recognise him…or did she? 'Sam! Goodness me, come in do.'

He stepped in and made to shake her hand. 'I should have come days ago, but business got the better of me. I apologise.'

'No apology needed. Aunt Ellie offered your services before speaking to you and I was afraid it was a terrible imposition but…'

He laughed. 'I know, nothing stops her when she's made her mind up.'

She showed him into the parlour and excused herself. Needing to run upstairs and straighten her hair. She sighed as she glanced in the mirror, she was wearing her shabbiest gown, knowing that she'd be at home working all day. She saw the truth in Georgie's bumpkin comment. Aunt Ellie had probably told the little cat Sam was coming this morning and Georgie had chosen not to warn her. They were both probably laughing at her now.

She took a breath before entering the room.

Sam jumped to his feet and she realised he was as tall and smart as her first impression suggested. He looked prosperous and scarily self-assured, but the corners of his eyes crinkled as he smiled widely and held out both his hands to her.

'Cousin Eliza.'

She returned the smile and placed her hands in his and they stood, smiling foolishly and drinking in the changes ten years had wrought. Her day took on an unexpected brightness. She cleared her throat and gently pulled her hands free.

He laughed awkwardly. 'Sorry. So stupid of me, but I have a picture of you in my mind. You were such a solemn girl, with your eyes fixed in a book or searching for your sisters. I know how idiotic this makes me sounds, but my goodness, you've changed. How long has it been?'

'Ten years. Sam, sit down and tell me what you've been doing.'

He entertained her with stories of his legal training in London and soon had her laughing as he described the fashions people in the city were wearing. There was an ease between them from the start with no hint of awkwardness that ten years of separation might have been expected to leave.

The Sam she remembered had been defensive and rude. He'd tagged behind Arthur and Freddy, copying their behaviour and agreeing with every word they uttered. When teased about his slavish devotion, he'd shown a fondness for using his fists that quickly ended his brief time as a figure of ridicule. She couldn't imagine him tagging behind anyone now.

Having brought each other up to date he turned to business. 'Tell me how I can help you?'

She told him what she'd learned since her meeting with the Givens family and admitted she was seriously considering taking a more active role in managing the family holdings.

'I have to. When Arthur told me the mother and baby home was my responsibility I realised how neglectful I'd been. There's the newspaper of course, although that take's care of itself. There's a patch of ground where a row of cottages once stood, locals use it for grazing. I know it was special to Ruby, but not why.'

He shook his head.

'What?'

'Well, I've heard things about Ruby, she was no angel you know.'

'She loved and provided for us, and she's your family too. If she made mistakes, who are we to judge her?'

He gave her an odd look, surprised respect, and she felt encouraged.

'I've just discovered there has been an offer made for the land, but I can't quite bring myself to consider selling it and I'm weak with relief that I know about it because I think the Givens men would have gone ahead and sold up. It might make sense to sell half of it but, I simply don't know.'

Sam put his hand up to slow her down. 'Sorry,' he said, clearing his throat. 'Half of what land?'

'That's exactly what I mean, there is so much for me to get to grips with that I'm not making myself plain. I'm sorry, I mean the old pleasure gardens, you know, Sansome Springs?'

'Oh, yes of course.' He looked at her in amazement. 'You've received an offer for it?'

'I've only just learned of it, although it was made to the Givens brothers some time ago. I shan't accept though. I have no business experience, but I'm not a fool and I won't be rushed into something I'm not comfortable with. I'm confident there will be a better offer forthcoming. Even then I may not sell.' She felt her cheeks redden.

'I expect I sound stupid, but I'm so confused about everything. There's so much that I know nothing about and I'm feeling a little overwhelmed.'

She realised Sam had paled and was looking blankly at her. "I'm sorry, I'm not explaining everything clearly. Let me send for...'

He waved his arm in denial. 'Not at all. I've been working very hard of late and my brain is a little tired. I was anxious to come and see you as soon as I was able to set your mind at ease, but I think I lost my concentration for a while. Forgive me.'

Eliza opened a window. 'It is horribly stuffy in here, sit quietly and I'll arrange for tea.'

Sam looked much better when she returned, he'd regained his colour and quickly stood to help with the trays she and Mary carried in.

'What a spread, I didn't expect you to go to all this trouble.' He said, beaming at Eliza.

'She didn't go to any trouble at all.' Mary replied crisply as she closed the door behind her.

Eliza grinned at Sam's shocked face. 'She's a treasure, really, she is.'

'Possibly better buried?' They laughed as she poured his tea, thankful that at least he had a sense of humour.

He sipped it slowly as his eyes fell on the pile of paperwork. 'It will take me time to get up to date with everything, but be assured, I shall offer you every assistance in managing your affairs. I'll be proud to guide you through the maze. We're family after all.'

Eliza gazed at him over the top of her tea cup and felt at last she had someone on her side.

'We must see to it that the right people are informed, should you decide to sell. If you do choose to go that way there'll be considerable interest, you can be sure of that. Do nothing in a hurry is my primary advice.'

She noticed a hint of uncertainty in him for the first time and reminded herself that he was only just qualified. 'Yes, of course. I'm in no rush Sam.'

'I'd like to take some time to look over this paperwork you seem to be buried in'. His eyes teased her.

'Why don't I take a pile of it along with me? I can study at home, in between setting up my office. I'll also take a visit out to Sansome Springs and get the lie of the land, literally. Bits of paper don't tell you everything.'

'What an unlawyerly thing to say!'

He laughed easily. 'Promise never to repeat that.'

'Tell me about the office you're setting up, you have plans to stay in Worcester?'

He nodded vigorously. 'I'm home for good and I'll need a place to hide when Ma gets too much.'

'She's good hearted.'

'Yes, a treasure, very much like your Mary.' The smile they shared made her blush.

'Really, I need to set up an office and get to work in earnest. Freddy and I hope to partner up. We're considering a couple of options, but nothing I can speak about just yet.'

CHAPTER THIRTY-FIVE

They both looked a little deflated when the door knocker rattled. They heard Mary mutter as she went to answer it, then muffled voices before the parlour door swung open to admit Alice, on a stream of fresh air and jumbled words.

'Mary said you were entertaining, but I knew you'd want me to come right in. Oh, is there tea? Wonderful.' She bent to kiss Eliza soundly on the cheek and then stood squarely in front of Sam who looked at her in surprise.

'We were talking business, but we can stop for tea.' He said.

Alice beamed happily. 'Oh, no need to break off because of me, we don't have secrets do we Eliza?'

Eliza shook her head. She didn't confide in her cousin as she used - their conversations of late now were very much devoted to James – but Alice was still her friend and she appreciated her sweet kindness.

Alice pulled up a small chair and dragged a side table closer, then loaded it with a brimming tea cup and a plate of cakes before sitting down with a contented sigh.

'Lovely to see you after so long Sam, have you found an office yet? Freddy tells us you have great plans. Tell me all.' She said, munching down on a very large slice of cake and groaning with pleasure.

'Mary hasn't lost her touch, this is delicious.'

Sam confirmed that he would be meeting a property owner later that day and expected to sign contracts for a place of his own within days. He then told them more of his time in London.

'You miss it already?' Alice asked.

'It's too soon to say, but Worcester is my home and I'll soon settle.'

Eliza picked up the conversation, telling Alice everything she'd discussed with Sam.

Alice listened attentively. 'Sansome Springs is shabby and uncared for and that's a shame. Now is probably the right time to release your capital and let someone else decide what to do with it.'

She smiled encouragingly at Eliza and then nodded toward Sam. 'It's fortunate that you have an abundance of cousins available to ensure you sell for a fair price and do the right thing with your money.'

Sam agreed. 'Indeed yes, I've reassured Eliza on that point, I shall treat her affairs as though they were my own.'

Alice raised her eyebrows. 'Lovely.'

He stood up and half bowed to them. 'I'll take my leave now, you have company and I have another appointment in town. I'll contact the man we spoke of and have a contract drawn up. We can get things started as soon as you feel ready. Would you allow me to take some of these and start working on them?' He indicated the bundles of papers piled in a corner.

Eliza kept her face straight, ignoring Alice, who was sending wide eyed glances and some very energetic nodding her way.

'Oh, Sam thank you. Not yet though, I want to go through everything myself first. We'll talk again when you've settled your own business, perhaps I shall visit you at your new office. It was so good to see you today and to know that you're going to help me.'

He nodded and bent to kiss her cheek.

She clapped her hands. 'I've just had a wonderful idea, now you're here, and all of Alice's brothers are at home, isn't it time for a grand reunion. Why don't the dozen cousins have a picnic on Sansome Springs?'

Alice clapped her hands excitedly. 'Oh yes, how lovely. Let's set a date now and I'll make sure all my brothers come. Do say yes Sam, it will be such fun?'

Sam nodded. 'Of course, I should love it.' He smiled at Alice. 'And I'll see to it that my brothers come too.'

Eliza kissed Sam's cheek. 'It's good to have you home Sam.'

'It's good to be home.' He clasped her hands and squeezed them, then turned to kiss Alice's cheek. 'Goodbye for now.'

The two women looked at each other with dancing eyes and held their breath as they listened to his retreating footsteps. Not until they heard the slam of the street door did they move, but then they jumped to their feet and hugged affectionately, cheek to cheek before Alice pulled away a little, arms still clasped around Eliza's waist.

'Well, that's a turn up. You invited the ghastly Pargeter boy for tea. I must say he seems to have turned out rather well.'

Eliza nodded, 'He did indeed.'

'I noted the goodbye kisses from both of you. Goodness me Miss Morgan, what would the neighbours think?'

'Alice!'

'I'm pleased that you have someone from the family helping you, I don't like the thought of you getting involved in the business but, you will be careful though, won't you? Don't forget, a Morgan is not fit to mingle with one of such high birth.'

Eliza chuckled. 'Don't be unkind, he was just an awkward boy then, and we were probably very silly girls. He seems to be ambitious which I admire, and goodness me, did you see those soft brown eyes?'

They giggled together and discussed other notable points about Sam's appearance before calming down.

'Anyway, I didn't invite him, Ellie sent him. She's as worried as you are about me taking over my own responsibilities and not having a man to help me. So now I have. But none of you need to panic, I won't be making any moves until I have a lot more knowledge, I know I can't afford to make a mistake.'

'Hmm.'

'Whatever happens I need to be friends with Sam, he's going to be an important man in Worcester one day and I may need the help of a lawyer somewhere down the line. I certainly couldn't turn to the Givens brothers, even in a pinch.'

Alice walked over and closed the window that had been opened for Sam. 'It's cold in here.' She pulled the heavy drapery closed, then open. She shifted an ornament from one side of the mantle to the other and then back again, then studied her reflection in the looking glass above the fire.

Eliza stood to the side of her allowing their eyes to meet in the mirror. 'What is it?'

Alice wanted to say something difficult and Eliza knew how much she hated anything uncomfortable and tried to pre-empt her.

'You really mustn't worry about my depending on Sam before I get to know him, I've learned my lesson by trusting the Givens' for as long as I have, I won't make that mistake again.'

Alice shrugged apologetically 'It's not just him. I worry about you taking on so much, that's all. The house, the twins, the library, all this business with Sansome Springs and the mother and baby home. I wonder how you'll cope with it all along with your problems with Emily?'

Eliza shook her head and looked at her cousin with a look that clearly said *what would you do?*

'What does Georgie say?' Alice asked.

'What we've always agreed. We're family and we'll stick together.'

'That's all well and good for her to say, but she's thinking of marriage and babies and will be leaving you and Emily here and you'll be missing out on everything. Have you told her about Peter? That he ran for the hills when he discovered that taking you meant also taking Emily?'

Eliza sighed. Every couple of months they went through a variation on this theme. She knew it was well meant, but it was so irritating.

'No. That's not Georgie's fault and she needn't worry about it.'

'I'm not suggesting it was anyone's fault, except his. It was entirely because he's a weak and selfish worm of a man. But even so, she should know that he ran out on you because of Emily, and the same thing could happen to her.'

Alice had braced herself to say what she wanted to and now she'd started she intended to finish. 'She should be helping you out more, you can't be expected to shoulder everything alone. You're locked away, seeing very little of anything but work and I'm so afraid no-one will offer for either of you. It's not fair to let her carry on this way.'

Eliza whirled around with tears in her eyes, she dashed them away angrily. 'Must we do this today Alice? She's my sister and I love her with all my heart so what am I supposed to do with her? Throw her out because she makes you uncomfortable, is that what you're asking me to do?'

Alice stepped back, hurt and shocked. 'That's a horrible thing to say. You're my dearest friends and I've never been uncomfortable with Emily. This isn't about me, it's about you and your future. I want you to have what every woman wants, marriage and a handful of children. I want Georgie to have the same chances, but I don't know how that will happen if you don't let someone else take care of Emily.'

'I can't send her away.' Eliza slapped the arm of her chair for emphasis. 'I won't send her away. She's gentle and loving, she asks for nothing and gives so much. The accident was not her fault and I won't allow her to be punished for it. I don't want to fall out with you, but if this continues I will. It seems as though everything I do is wrong to you. You're my friend and you should be on my side, but it doesn't feel as though you are.'

Alice blinked away a tear. 'I am on your side and I am your friend and that means telling you the truth. I'm sorry I've hurt you, I won't mention it again, I promise. I've said what I needed to.'

A silence hung heavy over them as they sat and thought about how close they'd both come to saying something unforgivable.

'Still friends?'

'Always friends.' A kiss and a reassuring hug and it was over. Until the next time.

CHAPTER THIRTY-SIX

'Alice tells me you're seeing a lot of Eliza.' Freddy said.

Sam looked up, eyebrows raised. 'Listening to girlish gossip? Your brain's gone soft, I'd thought better of you than that.'

'I like her Sam.'

'She's your sister, of course you do.'

'Dammit, I mean Eliza, don't play the fool. What are you up too?'

'I didn't push in, I was invited. She's my cousin and in need of help. While I'm trying to attract new clients, it won't hurt me to look out for her at the same time. It's all adding to my knowledge of what's what. That girl has a controlling interest in more than I imagined and yet she hasn't had the sense to turn any of it into income.'

He smiled and raised his hands. 'Here I am, ready to rescue her.'

Freddy felt the heat of anger rise even as his common sense told him to shut up and listen. Sam was ruthless, taking what he wanted and caring nothing for others and he'd closed his eyes to it. Worse than that, he'd joined in. They'd had some mad escapades in London and neither one was more to blame than the other. But now they were home Freddy didn't want to continue as before. He respected his Pa and wanted to make him proud, he loved his cousins and wouldn't see them hurt.

'Just remember she's a favourite of my Pa, so…'

'Christ, I'm not doing her down, I'm practising. She has assets that are not being maximised and I can help her. She'll profit from it. Now, forget all that, tell me about the school. Have you found the guts to talk to your Pa? Will he come up with the goods?'

Sam eyes narrowed at Freddy's expression.

'I did speak to him! The thing is, the school building is not actually ours you see.'

'Hah, he built it. I know it belongs to him. He's sold you a lie Fred, he knows you're soft and he's fobbed you off knowing you lack the stomach to fight for what you want my friend.'

The sneer was cutting, but not quite a threat.

'Come on Sam. Why would he lie? He's says he doesn't own it and I believe him.'

'Did you ask him who does own it?'

'Well…'

Sam's look of disgust sent a chill down his spine.

CHAPTER THIRTY-SEVEN

Eliza sighed in frustration as she realised the light was going, she'd been so engrossed in the mountain of paperwork that she'd lost track of time. She stood up, wincing as a twinge in the small of her back reminded her that this was the third day in a row she'd done nothing but sit and study.

Was she any further forward? Matching up Ruby's records with those she'd received from Messrs Givens showed a confusing picture. Whether that was intentional or down to her lack of experience, only persistence would tell.

She tapped her fingers together, her mind racing. Her account was being slowly bled of money and she thought she could see how they were doing it. Events had taught her to hold her tongue and think before doing anything and she hadn't got quite enough information to act yet. Going off too soon could be a mistake, there was much more to learn.

She heard the door behind her creak and guessed it was Mary, no-one else came in this room since she'd started this work. 'Bless you Mary, come and sit with me.'

They touched glasses as they surveyed the mess of paper strewn about the room.

'Making sense of it?'

Eliza nodded thoughtfully. 'I've been a fool, ignoring everything. I don't know what she'd think of me, I really don't.'

Mary snorted. 'She was no saint and she wouldn't expect you to be. You weren't ready before and you are now, that's all she'd think. Now don't get maudlin or I shan't give you another.'

Mary nodded to the bottle. 'Come on now, tell me what you've learned.'

'Well, I do own the birthing home and it's not being run the way Ruby intended. Women are being charged fees, but I can't see where they're going. Not into my account for sure.

'The newspaper is mine, though what on earth I'll do with it, I can't imagine. There is a plot of land near Bevere so perhaps I could sell that? A row of town houses – from which I see no sign of rental income - and this house.

'There's the gardens of course, and when we add that to the half share in Madame Eloise and the ladies lending library, well.' She exhaled heavily. I certainly don't see why we can't pay our bills.' She shook her head and looked dejected, but Mary jolted her shoulder none to gently.

'Get a hold of yourself girl. You'd have cause to cry if you'd just found out you were dirt poor. Seems to me, you've only got a thief to find and you'll be smiling and raising a glass to Ruby.'

Eliza smiled weakly. 'But what am I meant to do with it all?'

'Do what you want. Let's be honest, playing with all that she's left you will be a sight more fun than being married to that milksop you almost got yourself tangled up with.'

Eliza snorted and within minutes the two of them were laughing.

'Mary, why didn't you tell me about all this?'

Mary looked resigned. 'Me and Ruby were side by side as girls when we had nothing and did what we had to do to raise a crust. She was clever, I was loyal. She was always striving, I was content. I never cared what she had, I just did what I could to back her up when she had one of her mad schemes.

'She loved me too, mind you, but when it came to brains, she had enough for both of us. I couldn't keep up with her and I stopped trying.'

Mary smiled out into the middle of the room and then shook her head. 'Business was her pleasure not mine and now I hope it will be yours. I'll be there when you need me, but I don't want the details, that world don't interest me.'

Eliza nodded and then reached for a tattered bundle of paper that she'd set to one side. 'I found some letters from my father in amongst her papers. Do you remember him?'

Mary snorted. 'I remember Richard being born. She did the best she could for him, but it would never have been enough.'

She inhaled deeply then laughed. 'Do you know I've never said that before, but it's the truth. You only know him as your Pa, I only know him as her ungrateful son. He went away to school and came back thinking he was better than her, never mind that she worked every hour God sent to pay for his clothes and books and his schooling.

'He was a swine to her for years, blaming her for everything. I dared not say a word against him because she accepted the blame. She never forgave herself for not being what he needed you see. Whatever he said, she agreed with.'

Eliza sat in silence, she was weary, but Mary speaking in this unguarded way was unprecedented and she didn't want it to stop.

'She took on that blasted newspaper for him when he was just a boy, she paid nothing for it, mind. A friend of old man Daventor had been running it and he fell on hard times and turned to her for help. All that land used to belong to Ma Jebb, that was who Ruby worked for.

'She convinced Ma to let him move in to a couple of old cottages out there. They let him live and run his paper without paying rent. They did a partnership deal and she built it up into something Richard could work in and live off. No doubt it was her money that attracted that snotty wife of his.'

She paused then, remembering who she was talking to and then shrugged. 'Pah, it's time you knew the truth anyhow, your Ma was spoilt rotten and so was he, and I reckon all that bound them was Ruby's money, and the promise of more.'

Eliza's memory of her Mama had faded, but she'd clung on to the image of a perfect, angelic being and it was distressing to hear someone suggest otherwise, but she'd never known Mary to lie.

'It was a tragedy when she died, her and the baby, and I'm not saying otherwise. It was a wicked accident and I'm sorry for it. But for him to pack up and leave the three of you less than a month after, well, if Ruby could have found him she'd have killed him, and he'd have deserved it.

'He'd been gone more than a year before he wrote to her and by then she'd calmed down and seemed to understand why he'd left, although I never did. We never spoke of him again, she said she knew he wouldn't be back and talking about him caused her pain.'

Mary continued to stare into the centre of the room and the silence sat between them as Eliza poured them both another drink.

Eliza realised Mary had said all she would, for the time being at any rate. 'I think I understand him better now I've seen his letters. He wrote that the day they died he'd told her he was going away to fight in the war and they'd argued horrible. She'd been so angry she went out to spite him. Seeing us every day was a constant reminder that he killed our mother.'

Mary slapped her hand on her knee. She wasn't too tired to right a wrong when she heard one. 'Bull! He walked out the morning after she died, and spent the next month drinking and brawling and didn't set eyes on any of you. There was no constant reminder about it. He was as weak as water and couldn't face up to one half of what a man should face. He felt so guilty at leaving you three girls motherless he makes it right by leaving you fatherless too?'

Mary drank deeply and stood back up with a sigh. 'I'll tell you something I never could say before, you three are better off without him. He'd never have amounted to anything.'

Eliza picked up the little bundle of letters and smoothed them out carefully. 'He shouldn't have left us.'

'He should not, but he did. And now you have a powerful amount of work to be getting on with. Take hold of it and make it your own girl, no regrets and no fears.'

She glanced once more at the mountain of curled and yellowing paper and left Eliza to it.

CHAPTER THIRTY-EIGHT

MARY

Once she put her mind to it, Eliza got stuck in properly. I saw her, she read those papers again and again. She scribbled her notes, tore 'em up and scribbled some more.

Then she was off up the town. Talking to this one and that one and sending off messages here there and everywhere. The colour came back into her cheeks and her eyes sparkled. She didn't sleep much but she was looking better than she had for months.

She hardly noticed Georgie playing up or Arthur's comings and goings. It was almost like having Ruby back.

Of course, Sam is still oozing about the place and giving her the benefit of his wisdom, but I'm not too worried. She listens to him and seems charmed, but I know she's got a hefty dose of common sense and those robbing Givens brothers have taught her a lesson she won't forget, I hope.

I don't like him though. I haven't forgotten about his father and all that mucky business and I shan't hesitate to tell her, if I need to and it's no good Ellie Pargeter hoping I won't.

Eliza is my girl now and I'll tell her what I must to keep her safe, and I'm not above listening at doors if I think I should. Sly little bastard won't get one by us, I'll make sure of that.

CHAPTER THIRTY-NINE

The day of the picnic dawned bright and clear and Eliza greeted it optimistically, hoping a day away from the cursed papers might help clear her mind.

She'd have a chance to observe Sam with his cousins, which would be useful, but more importantly she'd be free to take a long and considered look at Sansome Springs. She knew it well, she'd played there as a child and had felt Ruby's passion for the place. Now though, she would be viewing the gardens in a different light.

Georgie and Emily walked ahead, giggling and whispering. At least she needn't worry about her passionate sister today. Nothing would upset Georgie, this was to be her first meeting with Freddy and she was bubbling with excitement and determined to be as sweet and dazzling as she possibly could.

In complete contrast to her mood of the previous week. She'd driven everyone mad, and worked herself into a state of near hysteria, intensified because she couldn't share what she was feeling with her twin.

Eliza recognised that Georgie was moving into a world that Emily would never understand. She wanted marriage and her own home and was thoroughly enjoying the multitude of young men offering her the world. She wanted, more than anything, to share these precious moments with her twin, but it was all beyond poor Emily who was fixed forever, young and innocent.

Emily sensed the change in her twin and struggled to understand, she'd become clingy and tearful whenever she was confused or if she felt she wasn't getting Georgie's undivided attention.

Georgie glanced back at Eliza now with a glorious smile and smoothed out the ribbons that flowed from the neck of her dress and then did the same for Emily who wore an identical gown, both pleased with the effect they created.

Eliza had questioned their choice of outfit earlier. 'We're going to be walking outside on damp grass, you'll ruin those shoes and stain your dress, won't you change into something more durable?'

'I want to look pretty for my cousins and anyone else I might meet.' She looked Eliza up and down, clearly not impressed with her choice of outfit.

'It might have been nice if you'd made more of an effort, why must you always be so dull. People will assume you're our maid if you follow us dressed like that.'

Eliza raised her eyebrows, but didn't bother to respond, Georgie was a master at tossing out a cutting phrase, but she was determined nothing would spoil this outing.

They'd had cross words the other day when Eliza had caught Georgie simpering around Sam and making him blush.

'I can't imagine what you said to make a sophisticated man like him react that way but whatever it was, you shocked him Georgie.'

Georgie had stormed out and Eliza had been too distracted, and a little afraid of what she might learn, to resume their conversation. She considered asking Sam what had occurred between them, but decided, least said, soonest mended.

She realised that Georgie was leagues ahead of her in terms of sophistication but was at a loss as to whether her sister was forward, or she backward.

Ana had told her not to worry, girls become women when they're ready and nothing can speed up or slow down the process and she accepted that. She had enough to worry about, without looking for more.

When they reached the agreed meeting place they were enveloped in a flurry of kisses and greetings from the cousins already gathered.

'Freddy's coming by boat, with Nate.' Alice chirped.

'Oh good, let's head over to the dock and meet them.' Georgie said, turning sharply away and heading for the landing stage.

'Hi Georgie, it's good to see you too.' Si, Sam's younger brother, laughed as Georgie sailed passed him without a glance.

She tossed a grin back at him but kept walking.

Eliza and Alice linked arms and walked together, flanked by Percy and Gabe. She and Arthur exchanged nods, breakfasting together negated the need for effusive greetings. They set off in Georgie's wake ready to greet Freddy and his brother.

Eliza narrowed her eyes and watched as the boat approached and then bounced gently into the dock. Nate jumped to land first and turned to extend a helping hand to Freddy, who laughed and hopped to the shore unaided and uncaring of his smart jacket and glossy boots.

He smiled at Eliza as though they were old friends, and she smiled back, resolutely ignoring Georgie's jealous glare. He hailed Sam casually, then glanced up at his cousins, all waiting to welcome him home. He removed his hat and swept a huge bow to them.

'Oh, do hurry up Fred, everyone wants to see you and I'm ready to eat.' Alice had her sister-in-charge voice ready.

Freddy nodded and walked up the bank and, at the same time, Georgie stepped forward, ensuring she was the first one he saw face to face. Her smile was dazzling.

Freddy stood still, as though in shock, and flicked his head back and forth between Emily and Georgie several times. 'Good lord, can this be the two naughty little girls I remember from school? I must say you've grown up very nicely.'

He lightly kissed them both on the cheek, cuffed Matty gently on the shoulder and turned to shake Si's hand, who then passed him on to Eliza.

He bent to kiss her, as he had her sisters and then pulled back. 'Eliza.'

Alice stepped forward. 'Come on, let's find some shade and get settled.

'Well, I don't think he spared her more than a glance. Is she going to be upset?' She whispered to Eliza.

Eliza looked around to be sure they weren't being overheard and, catching Freddy's eye, she turned quickly back to Alice.

'Livid, but I don't blame him. The poor man has come home to start a new life. He's not going to be interested in a besotted cousin, not until he's found his feet. I hope she'll behave this afternoon, but she rarely gives up without a fight.'

Georgie confounded her by being as charming as she'd ever been, she chattered to everyone and handed round food and drink and was a perfectly sweet girl.

'Arthur's so caught up in his work I'm surprised he took the time to come and eat with us today. He'd never take an entire day off but, this is good enough. And at least now he's staying at your house we can relax, knowing he's eating well and sleeping in a decent bed. Do you see very much of him?' Alice asked.

Eliza had caught Freddy's eyes again and her stomach flipped. Was he watching her? She turned away and saw Sam looking her way and was thrown into confusion. Freddy and Sam had added colour and confusion to her world.

She eased back and smiled, thoroughly enjoying being surrounded by family and eager to get to know them better. It was a comforting feeling.

'Eliza, where are you?' She felt an elbow in her ribs.

'Sorry, I'm dreaming.' She smiled. 'What was that?'

'Oh, it was just chatter.' Alice considered her flushed face and shining eyes. 'I must say, you're looking very well, there's a glow about you that is good to see.'

Eliza leaned forward and held both of Alice's hands in hers, 'I'm learning so much and it's all such a thrill. I'm quite cross that I waited so long to get myself involved but maybe the time wasn't right. And at least I've managed to lift one burden from Arthur's shoulders, he was correct when he told me there was profiteering going on at the mother and baby home. I'm going to make it my first job, to change the way things are done out there, and I'll make sure nothing like that ever happens again.'

Alice cleared her throat. 'Should you personally get involved though? I do wish you'd take my advice and appoint a manger to run things the way you want. Business in general is bad enough, but that is not the thing for you to be too close to. You must consider how it would appear to outsiders. Most of those women have no husbands you know.' She hated disagreements but couldn't keep silent when a thing had to be said but the distress was clear on her face.

'Oh, listen to yourself Alice. My agents are the ones who are allowing the profiteering to occur, how can you expect me to put someone else in charge and risk the same thing happen again? I'll talk to Sam before I do anything, I promise.'

Alice squirmed, but she wouldn't back down. 'But those women, I know they're unfortunate and must be helped, but surely you understand? Wrongs should be righted, but must they be righted by you? You seem so strident, and it's disconcerting. I'd hate for you to be misunderstood.'

'Hmm. Strident and mixing with dubious women. Well, I'm not as offended by that description as you might expect. I rather think it accurate so there's little danger of me being misunderstood. Now, the others are approaching, is there anything else you want to criticise me for before they get within hearing distance? I'd like to keep your poor opinion of me between us.'

Alice looked shocked and tears sparked in her eyes. 'I didn't say that, Eliza!'

Eliza smiled sadly, they'd been falling out so much recently. They always made up, but each time it happened the gulf got wider. It hurt badly, but there was little she could do to stop it.

'But a part of you thought it. I'm changing, or maybe I'm discovering who I really am. I feel as though I've been wasting time waiting for something to happen and now I'm going out and making it happen. The new me might take some getting used to, but don't lose faith in me. I can feel the difference and I promise it won't spoil our friendship, but it may change it. I still depend on you.'

Alice nodded. She'd wanted to talk more about her love affair with James but felt horribly reluctant to mention him to her newly fierce friend. 'I won't lose faith in you, but don't leave me behind.'

'Alice, I'll never leave you behind. Heavens, I love you more than I love my sisters some days, and I certainly trust you more than I trust them. I know I'm doing things you disapprove of but I'm not going to stop. I'm sorry I've neglected you recently, and I can't swear I won't do it again. I seem to lose myself for days trying to find the right path to follow, but I'll always come back. Now, quickly, tell me the latest about the handsome James and your continuing abandonments. I trust there have been more stolen moments?'

Alice's face lit up and Eliza was pleased. She did love her dearly, Alice had been a saviour when Ruby had died. Steadfast and loyal, she'd held her hand as she cried and then hastened to reassure her that she could manage.

She should try to be kinder to Alice despite the differences that were appearing between them. It struck her that she'd spent so long fretting about the changes in Georgie and how they'd effect Emily, but she'd entirely overlooked the fact that she and Alice were experiencing that very thing. How painful it was when one grew and the other didn't.

She watched Alice's face now, glowing with love as she recounted her latest meeting with James and resolved to do all she could to protect Alice's innocence, while still following her own path.

Encouraged by Eliza's attention Alice prattled happily on about James and her confidence that he felt the same way about her, until they were disturbed by the laughter of the others, ready for their lunch.

CHAPTER FORTY

Eliza scrutinised the picture that lay on the table beside her then looked uncertainly at her sister's hair. She made a minor adjustment, stepped back to view the results, shook her head and re-adjusted the curls.

She put down the comb and sighed with relief when Georgie smiled.

It had been hard work, but all in all she'd done a pretty good job copying the intricate hair style that they'd admired in one of the fashion periodicals Sam had given them.

Helping each other with their hair was a new development since Georgie requested they have a maid to assist with clothes and hair. Eliza had laughed until she cried then surprised them both by coming up with a compromise.

The intimacy of these shared moments fostered a warmer understanding than any they'd known before. It was a great deal of work because whatever style she managed for Georgie had to be duplicated for Emily and this ate into her free time, but the improvement in their relationship made it worthwhile.

'You look lovely.'

Georgie preened and turned her head from side to side. 'I do, don't I.'

It was a statement not a question and Eliza smiled. She'd done a far better job than she'd thought she would when Georgie first waved the pamphlet from London in front of her.

'We must arrange another lunch with our cousins, the last one was fun wasn't it?' Eliza said.

Georgie, still admiring herself, nodded. 'Hmm, Freddy didn't pay much attention to me, he seemed distant, but I expect that was because there were so many of us together after so long. It was lovely seeing them all, and hearing their news, although Sam is here as often as Arthur recently.'

She glanced at Eliza's face but there was no hint of a blush on her smiling face.

'I expected it would be like being back at school, but I felt I was at a party with strangers. Do you know what I mean?'

'Mmm. Because we were together as children that's how we remember them and it's how they remember us too. It was strange, the way we were all looking at each other and then looking again to see how we've changed. I don't want us to drift any further apart though.'

'Do you think Freddy liked me?'

Eliza sighed, it always came back to this. 'Georgie, he's your cousin, of course he did. I wish you could be happy with what you've got, you're making yourself miserable and irritating me.'

'Do you like him?'

'Yes, I like him. But he's just a man.'

Georgie placed her hands over Eliza's and their eyes met in the mirror. 'I know I'm not clever like you and I don't mind that. You're going to be happy, working and arranging things and refusing to fall in love, but I'm entirely different. I like being admired for my looks and being spoiled and looked after, and I want that to continue, but I want a man to do it.'

Eliza pulled a face and Georgie smacked her gently on the hand. 'You might not care about finding a husband but if you keep pulling faces like those you'll get wrinkles on your face, you'd care about that.'

Eliza gasped in horror and leaned close to the mirror to inspect her face.

Georgie continued. 'Don't you really wish you were married though? And don't pinch your mouth like that, you really have got wrinkles there.'

Georgie laughed. 'Men want a bit of sweetness you know. You always seem so sour, I'm certain that's why you lost the only admirer you had.'

She looked frankly at her sister's face. 'You're quite plain, and if you don't have a smile on your face you can look grim.'

Eliza flushed and her eyes smarted.

'I'm sorry, but you don't hold back when upsetting me is for my own good, and now I'm telling you. You're not too old to find a man, but you must try harder. Everyone was so charming at the picnic, but you sat in the background, huddled up with Alice like a couple of old maids.'

For some reason this, more than her other comments stung Eliza. 'I'm not looking for a man, but if I were it would not be a fashion plate like the ones you seem attracted too.'

'You mean Sam and Freddy?' Georgie's voice had a note of outrage in it.

Eliza found herself wishing she was prettier and that she had some nicer clothes and she was cross with herself. 'Yes, I mean them.

'You made a fool of yourself giggling and fawning over them like a silly child. That sort of behaviour is not for me.'

'And yet I'll have an offer, if not two, in no time! And you'll be left here as a fusty spinster and it will be your own fault.'

'You think they are…?

Eliza went cold. She was confused and angry with herself. Those two ridiculous men with their London gloss had come back and thrown everything into disarray. She didn't know what she thought about anything anymore and every time she closed her eyes she saw one of them smiling at her.

Georgie dropped to her knees and clasped Eliza's hands, pulling her back to the here and now. 'Don't be angry with me Eliza. I'm not like you, I don't want to be in charge and to have to worry about everyone else. I want someone to take care of me. I like being pretty and I like having pretty things. Is that so bad?'

Eliza stroked her hands through Georgie's shining hair and twisted the fresh curls around her finger. 'I'm not angry with you. I'm concerned because you feel things so passionately and are then crushed when things don't go your way. I'd hate to see you badly hurt, but you can't make someone love you, they either do or they don't.' She smiled. 'There are more important things to worry about anyway.'

'Such as?'

'Pink and swollen eyes from persistent sulking.'

Georgie smiled.

CHAPTER FORTY-ONE

Eliza's eyes sparked out a warning as she approached the offices of Givens and Givens. She'd been diligent since the lawyers had visited her and now she was ready to fight, if she must.

She marched through the plush waiting room and rapped smartly on the inner door but walked right in without waiting for a response. The clerk and one of the Mr Givens were in conference and both looked shocked at the intrusion.

'Mr Givens, we need to talk.'

He shuffled the pile of papers that were laid out on the table and tried to muster a smile. 'This is a private meeting Miss Morgan, I must ask you to wait in the lobby.'

She waved her hand airily 'This won't take a minute. I've decided to bring our business relationship to an end. Examination of the reports you gave me - patchy though they were – show me that your family has been earning more from my interests than I have. I can see why, from your point of view, that is satisfactory. You'll understand that it's a little less so from my perspective.'

Both Mr Givens and the clerk gaped at her.

She smiled and then rapped on the desk. 'Come along now, gentlemen, I'm very busy. I need the papers that you retained, and I'd like you to sign this.'

Mr Givens read the sheet of paper she'd placed before him and shook his head. 'I can't sign that, and you can't dispense with us in this manner.'

She shrugged. 'It would be convenient if you signed now, but it's not essential. Everyone has been informed that you are no longer acting on my behalf and you'll find no more of my money trickling in to your coffers. Good day.'

It took Mr Givens a moment to gather his wits, but he followed. 'Miss Morgan, if there has been a misunderstanding I apologise. Won't you return to the office where we can go over everything again?'

She stepped into the sunshine that bathed the street and blessed him with a radiant smile. 'No, Mr Givens. As I said, our business is at an end. If you'd be so kind as to release the documents you have relating to my holdings by the end of this week, we'll leave it at that.'

'Impossible at such short notice. We'll need to…'

She took a deep breath. 'I turned to you for help and advice but rather than treat me with respect you tried to bully me in a clumsy attempt to distract me. It failed, you've been mismanaging my business and I've appointed a new legal team. If you fail to return my documents, you can convey your excuses directly to the magistrate.'

She left him gaping.

CHAPTER FORTY-TWO

'I'd like to walk with you this morning Arthur, if I may? I have a situation you may be able to help me with.'

He nodded, but rather than abandon his breakfast as he had a few months ago, hastily poured himself another cup of coffee. He felt completely at home, and, when he managed to be there for breakfast he made the most of it. He was not going to be rushed out today, the memory of that dreadful tea room still made him shudder.

Eliza sat back down cheerfully enough, happier in his company now that they'd reached an understanding. It had taken a nasty row to do it, but they'd both spoke their minds, and both went to bed with some home truths ringing in their ears.

She told him to shut up when he became pompous and he ignored her when she became bossy, and despite her aunt's plotting, they'd fallen into a comfortable brother, sister relationship that suited them both.

'You can talk in here if privacy is what you want. I'm going in early, we're experimenting.' Georgie opened the door and flounced out.

'The little cat could have said earlier,' Eliza muttered.

'I find the thought of her and Ellie conducting experiments unsettling.'

'Oh, heavens, they'll survive.' She dismissed them from her mind. 'Do you remember when you told me about the mother and baby home, you said you'd heard about it from a decent family who were having hard times?'

He nodded. 'The Barker's, yes, it's a tragic story.'

'I'd like to hear it.'

He looked at her for a moment and saw that she was serious.

'Very well. Meg, their daughter, was walking home from work after dark and was attacked by a group of lads. They roughed her up a bit, stole her bag and left her. She'd have recovered with little harm done, but one of them went back, he pretended he was sorry and wanted to help. She's a sweet girl, naïve. She was tearfully grateful, and she let him lead her to the path where he forced himself on her.'

Eliza gasped, but nodded for him to continue

He sighed sadly. 'She managed to get home and her mother tended to her... when her time was near her mother took her to the home for help and they were turned away because they couldn't pay the fees.'

Eliza nodded thoughtfully. 'How do you know they're a decent family?'

'He was an assizes clerk at the Guildhall, he was one of the fellows who got hurt when the ceiling fell in, you'll remember that?'

Eliza nodded. 'Yes, I do. A half dozen or more men were trapped for a day or more. It was a miracle that they all got out alive.'

Arthur nodded. 'Alive, but badly injured. He was forced to stop work, Janet takes in laundry and does a bit of sewing, her money kept them going until her daughter's trouble. Meg got an infection and was on the point of death when they called me in. I was lucky, the girl lived and so did her little boy. They fed me and told me what had happened. I go back and see them every few months. They're finding life a struggle, but they're coping.'

'He's not back working?'

Arthur curled his lip in disgust. 'He lost his sight in the accident and the council have no use for a blind man.'

'Will you take me with you, the next time you visit them?'

He looked at her in amazement. 'They live in St Andrews, it's not… yes of course. I'd like to go one day next week. I'll let you know.'

'Thank you. I have an idea and, when it's clearer in my mind you'll be the first to know.'

The clock in the hall chimed and they both jumped to their feet and dashed through the door, he to the infirmary and she to the library.

CHAPTER FORTY-THREE

If ever she stopped to think, Eliza might be afraid she'd bitten off more than she could chew, but she felt energised and productive. The time for thinking was over.

She'd been incensed to discover that she was losing money in a couple of areas, more through laziness than dishonesty.

The paltry amount the Givens men had been trickling into their own account was a drop in the ocean. If they'd only swallowed their arrogance and been nicer to her they'd have been earning from her for years to come.

The manager of the mother and baby home had been collecting fees while starving the place of funds. Knowing she'd stopped their game was gratifying, and they would pay, just as soon as she worked out how to make that happen.

In the meantime, there was a frightening shortfall in their account and she could think of only one way to make that up. She irritably pushed the papers aside and stood up to stretch as she performed her usual checks in preparation for going to bed.

After bolting the door and closing the window shutters she turned to shake Mary, who sat in the fireside chair, head on one side and snoring like a hog.

An empty bottle lay at her feet and Eliza guessed she'd had a drop more than was good for her. She'd wake up cold and uncomfortable if she was left, despite how comfortable she looked now.

She touched the sleeping woman on her shoulder. 'Time for bed Mary. I'll help you up.'

Mary groaned and pulled herself up right easing her stiff neck and wiping her face with her hands. 'Not yet lovey, I've been waiting to have a little natter with you. Let's have a drop of something and I'll tell you what's on my mind.'

Eliza waited with interest to see what Mary had to say, she rarely offered an opinion on anything even when asked. *You've got a better brain than me girl. You decide what you want to do, I'll back you up.*

Mary had never gone against Ruby in life, and since her death, had never gone against Eliza.

The older woman sighed and stretched out her legs, twisting her ankles till they popped. 'They're a mixed bunch, those Daventors and you need to be on your guard... not about your sister though. Hugh... is a good man, that we all know for sure. But Hugh's father, he was a bad lot.' She exhaled loudly.

'My mind's playing tricks on me, I think the old man was Hugh's uncle, not his father. Don't matter, the point is there's good and bad in that family.'

'Mary, I...'

'Dammit let me finish girl. You're always in such a blasted hurry. Why can't you wait and let a story unfold in its own time?

'I don't know whether Freddy will turn out to be a decent fellow like his father or a bastard like his grandfather, that's the point I'm trying to make. He could go either way. I've heard you trying to put Georgie off him and you should save your breath.

'If she fancies herself in love with him, you keep trying to change her mind she'll dig her heels in, you know what a cussed creature she is. If you could just let it alone she'd fancy herself in love with another fellow next week.

'She's a twit, but she's a Morgan and they do hate being told what to do. She's ready for a husband and she'll go against you if you try to stop her. You'd do better to let her go and get what she wants, and then do the same for yourself.

'Your head's spinning, you want to work on the business and you want to be courted. It's natural and if Freddy prefers you to your sister that's not your fault and there's no changing it.'

'Nonsense, I've never…'

'Shush, I'm talking. You've got Freddy making eyes at you which is entertaining as all hell because I can see you're not enthralled by him, though your daft sister is. You and Freddy! No good would come of that. Then there's Sam sniffing around and one thing I can tell you for certain, his father was a wrong un. Not that Ellie would ever admit that.'

'Mary, that's unfair, he can't be blamed for what his father may have done.'

'Hah. Apples and trees, my girl, apples and trees. My point is, you're worrying about what your sister might do, and not noticing what's happening to you. You've half a dozen businesses earning money that you don't see a penny of and yet still you're walking around worrying about her. Now whether that's because you don't know what to do, or because you're afraid of doing it, I don't know, but you're running out of time.

'Sit down and think about what's important to you, forget the rest. And remember this, God won't strike you down if you dare to have fun at the same time as you do your work.'

Eliza made no attempt to interrupt, Mary was clearly still as sharp as she had ever been. Did the woman miss nothing?

'But what will I do when Georgie realises that Freddy doesn't want her?'

Mary shook her head. 'Nothing. That's not your business. It happens every day to somebody and they live, she will too. She's a grown woman and let's be honest, we both know ambition drives her, not love. She's unbreakable and in no danger of coming off worse in a failed love affair. I've kept my mouth shut, not being family...'

Eliza disputed this. 'You *are* family and you always will be. I am worried about Georgie, her passion for Freddy was sweet when she was little, but now she won't allow herself to back down.'

Mary nodded, as though to say *at last*. 'That's my point, you're worrying about her even when you know she's playing a part. Open your bloody eyes, you've got more important things to be working on.

'She'll cause you problems for the rest of her life if you let her. You need to work on your own and Emily's future. Now bugger off and let me get to my bed.'

CHAPTER FORTY-FOUR

Eliza had noticed a gradual change in John and Jacob, a cooling off almost. They'd been a warm and reassuring presence in her childhood and she was sad to see that warmth cooling.

'It'll be because you're the boss, no doubt.' Ana had suggested.

But she knew it was more than that, they'd been happy enough for a long time, recently something had altered. It was irritating, she didn't have time to be smoothing ruffled feathers. Business was business and she needed them to stop whatever it was that was distracting them.

She opened the office door and John looked up with a smile that didn't reach his piercing blue eyes. 'John, how are you?'

He nodded toward the press. 'We're keeping ourselves busy.'

'Well, I haven't come to get in your way, but I would like to talk to you so, would you prefer to do that now or shall we arrange another date?'

'You're here, I'm here, let's do it now.' He sighed heavily. 'I imagine you're here to tell me we're closing down, is that it?'

She looked at him blankly 'Closing down what?'

'Everything we've worked for. I'm not ungrateful mind, this newspaper has given us an education and a living, but I'll be sorry to leave it. Tell you the truth, Jacob was here but when he saw you coming he ducked out the back window. He struggles to keep his mouth shut and he wouldn't want to be rude to you.'

'Well, I appreciate the courtesy but…' Eliza shook her head in confusion. 'I'm not closing the newspaper or taking anything away from you. I can't imagine what would happen here without you, both of you. What on earth made you think that I would?'

He flushed beet red. 'We've got contacts all over the city, finding out what's going on is our business, after all. A fellow said he knows of a chap who reckons all of this, and the library was to be sold off. You're closing the newspaper because it's not showing the returns you want. The whole lot is to be levelled and something new built here.'

Her eyes flashed. 'And who is this knowledgeable man?'

'Couldn't say. Folks tell me things, knowing I won't press for more than they want to give.'

She sighed impatiently. 'Yes, of course, but really, its utterly ridiculous. You know better than anyone else that we're profitable and have been for years. Why would you believe something that a stranger says before talking to me?'

He shuffled awkwardly and looked about as though hoping to be rescued. 'We figured you'd probably got bad memories of this place and nobody could blame you, what with the accident and all.'

'Well, I promise you I have no intention of closing this newspaper or the library. It's time to put an end to this nonsense, I do have plans but you're an important part of them, can you call Jacob back? We three need to talk.'

CHAPTER FORTY-FIVE

Spending hours each week with Sam, poring over the accumulation of paperwork proved to be an invaluable education. He had a clear way of thinking that helped her focus on what was important and not get side tracked by minor irritations.

She read every line and listened to every word of advice and was beginning to see how she wanted things to be. She was free of the history and loyalties that had been Ruby's. This was her world now and she had an expensive family to care for.

She'd managed to clear the day to day debts and her confidence grew with each settled account. She was now anxious to dispose of whatever holdings she could. They represented her income, but not her dreams, and she found viewing them that way enabled her to move forward.

Sam frequently disagreed with her but, after making his point, followed her instructions to the letter and she thought they were building a good working relationship.

'I want the Barker's to move into the mother and baby home as soon as their quarters can be made ready. Where are we on that?'

He flicked through the documents on his desk and then reached behind to pull something else forward. 'Ah, here it is. Another week and it will be ready. It's taken some time because you're giving them a much bigger plot than the last family had.'

'They'll need it, I've told them they must aim for self-sufficiency. They can work the land, with the help of the women and feed themselves.'

He shook his head, he'd known that was her intention, but he disagreed at every opportunity. 'If you made every woman pay a fee, the job would be done. I don't see your problem with that. Anything else will cost you and that's bad business.'

She shook her head stubbornly. 'It always paid for itself in the past and there's no reason it can't be made to do so again. The library can give them a little money to get them started. They'll sell the produce they don't use. You'll see.'

'Maybe so, but it won't earn you anything.' He couldn't understand why she refused to see the obvious.

'For goodness sake Sam, not everything is about profit. The home is a blessing for women in need and I want it to continue to be that. All the time that beastly man, in collusion with Givens' was making women pay, my account was supporting them. Wickedness.' She slapped her hand on the table for emphasis.

Sam raised his hands in submission. 'It's your business, but it's my duty to tell you what I think, and now I've done it. The Barkers will be installed next week. Shall we move on?'

'Certainly. What's next?'

'The contract for John and Jacob is prepared, exactly as you specified. I urge you to sleep on your decision and only then sign it. This is a step that can never be reversed. I hope you'll reconsider.'

She took the contract from him. She'd happily sign now, but it was important that Sam felt he had some power of persuasion with her. It would set his mind at ease if he thought there was chance that she'd think better of the scheme.

'Any thoughts on selling that patch of land?'

She tapped the table and pictured Sansome Springs. She'd had a decent offer for a large portion of the land and she was almost resigned to the inevitable. It needs so much work and I need capital, I don't see any choice.'

The costings to turn the pleasure gardens into something the public would pay to visit were impossible for her to risk. 'I need to think about it, it's a huge step to take and I don't want to make a mistake, that land was important to Ruby.'

Sam sniffed. His disdain for Ruby had come as shock to her at first, but she'd put it down to a childhood prejudice he'd never grown out of and barely noticed it now.

'She didn't leave things in good order you know, there's a mess to sort out. I'll help all I can, but you must act soon.'

'I know Sam. Is there anything else?'

'I've had an enquiry from a chap interested in the empty school building, nothing certain yet but I'll let you know.'

She looked up, blank. 'What are you talking about?'

Sam raised his eyebrows. 'Our old school. It's empty and in need of work. I know someone who might take it off your hands. I've...'

'But, no. That's not mine.' She was honestly confused. 'What made you think it might be?'

His jaw clenched, and she saw a flash of distrust in his eyes, gone almost as soon as it had appeared. 'The fellow that would like to take it over was certain. He's got it wrong, clearly.'

CHAPTER FORTY-SIX

Sam was a regular attendee at the Morgan suppers, and barely caused any excitement, but when Freddy showed up Georgie and her little band of gigglers were almost overcome. Fortunately, Aunt Ellie was on hand to whisper some calming advice in her ear, which prevented her from making a complete fool of herself.

Freddy was his normal, cheerfully debonair self. He circled the room, carefully speaking to everyone present before sitting down to play cards with Emily. Within the space of half-an-hour he earned himself a room full of friends. He even jumped up to help Mary with a loaded tray and laughed at her grumbles.

'No, please, you're our guest.' Eliza protested.

He took the weight of the tray and carried to the table. 'I'm family, don't stand on ceremony with me.' He shot a derisory glance at the girls who were watching him and whispering. 'I can't bear it when they fawn, and I won't accept it from you.'

'I promise to never fawn over you and I doubt I could giggle like that if my life depended on it. You're safe with me.'

'Thank heavens.' He smiled at her.

She felt a warm glow but refused to fall under his spell. He was too attractive for his own good. 'Why come to this sort of thing if you don't want to be…charmed?'

He smiled into her eyes and she felt the heat rise. He squeezed her hand, 'I wanted to see you, Eliza.'

Her laughter was genuine and infectious. 'Oh, please. I promised not to fawn, and now you must promise not to flirt, surely we have no need for that nonsense?'

'I'm sorry, I did it automatically. It's the type of thing that's expected… No more about London. All fawning and flirting between us is at an end. I'll go and mingle as a good guest should, but I'll see you again before I leave.'

She spent the rest of the evening being an attentive hostess, but she couldn't stop the warmth in her cheeks when she thought about his words. She hugged them to herself even as she told herself to grow up.

When Sam and Georgie put their heads together she felt a lick of concern but had seen in truth in Mary's warning, she was a Morgan and she'd do as she pleased.

Eliza turned away. Keeping her emotions hidden and her thoughts to herself was a new habit but she'd mastered it. She'd realised that very few people could, or would, put the needs of others before their own and if she was to get ahead, that's what she'd need to do.

CHAPTER FORTY-SEVEN

Georgie dashed the crystal hairpin dish to the floor, causing a satisfying crack. 'Why does he keep watching you? Isobel said he didn't take his eyes off you all evening.' She'd clearly been stewing on her jealousy ever since.

'If you screech at me one more time I'll slap you, and don't you dare throw anything else! Freddy and I are friends and we…'

'I don't want to know what you do! I just want you to stop doing it. He treats me like a child and it makes me so angry.'

'He treats you like a child because that's how you behave. You can't seriously think a grown man would chose to be with someone who still stamps her feet if she can't have her own way. You pout and sulk and twirl your hair like a ten-year old. You're extremely boring and you need to do something about it.'

Georgie's tears dried instantly as she gasped in outrage. 'Me, boring? You're the boring one.'

Eliza flung out her arms in a gesture of helplessness. 'I told you not to build your hopes up on a dream.'

'Is he in love with you?'

'No. For goodness sake, we're cousins, we're of an age and we share a sense of humour. We're both trying to find our way in the world and we have a lot to talk about. There's nothing more than that on my side. I hope that's all it is for him but, if he does have feelings for me, there's nothing I can do about that.'

Georgie folded her arms and looked mutinous although Eliza noticed there were no real tears. 'Yes, there is. You can tell him you're not in love with him.'

It was not surprising Georgie struggled to grow up when her closest friend, Emily, would be forever a child, and her most trusted adviser was Ellie who was a romantic fool, by sometimes Eliza wanted to scream at her.

'Would that make him love you? You know it wouldn't. How often do you comment on the differences between us, how dull and provincial I am in comparison to you, so fashionable and bright?'

'What do you mean by that?' Georgie's eyes were cold.

'Is it possible that after five years in London, Freddy may have had all the fashionable sophistication he wants? Perhaps he's hoping for a simpler life now he's home.'

Georgie shook her head, dismissing the very thought. 'You've always envied me. I see what you're trying to do, and I'll hate you for taking the only thing I ever wanted.' She ran from the room, slamming the door so hard the windows rattled.

Eliza dropped onto the seat, hating the unpleasantness, but relieved that matters had come to a head. Georgie would be unbearable for a few days, but the storm would pass, as it needed to.

Having spent time with Freddy, Eliza knew without any doubt that Georgie would drive him to distraction within hours. She'd seen his grimace of distaste at all the fluttering before supper. He viewed Georgie as a tedious child.

CHAPTER FORTY-EIGHT

Eliza smiled hesitantly at the vaguely familiar woman standing on her doorstep. She didn't know her, but she'd seen her about town, she was sure.

'You must be Eliza, I'd recognise you anywhere.'

'I'm sorry, I can't place you.'

'No reason why you should my lovely. I hope you'll invite me in though, I hate to give the neighbours gossip fodder.' Her wide smile didn't reach her eyes.

Eliza reluctantly stepped back and opened the door wide. 'Come in and tell me how I can help.'

'I don't know that it's help so much as doing the right thing. You don't know me, but I know all about you and your pretty sisters. And Ruby of course, who died and left you all alone to fend for yourself.

The prickles up Eliza's back were getting sharper. 'Who are you?'

'Ah, you might call me Mrs Morgan, but as we're family Mama will do. I married your dear Papa.'

The woman walked across the hallway and opened the parlour door. 'This is cosy, shall we sit and be comfortable?'

Eliza was speechless.

'I know I must be a surprise for you dear but do come in and sit down like a lady. I've been content to watch over you girls from a distance, but circumstances have changed. You're about to get yourself into trouble and I owe it to your Papa to step in and help.'

She scanned the room impatiently. 'Is there a bell to ring, I really would like some tea?'

CHAPTER FORTY-NINE

MARY

I'll have to think about this very carefully.

Someone's trying to pull something over on us, but I can't work it all out and Eliza's that fired up if I speak I could cause her to go off hot headed.

I remember Richard Morgan and I'm bloody sure he wouldn't have married a type like that. Musty gown and grubby fingernails, with a voice that's as put on as Georgie's tears.

And she turns up wanting her share, just after my girl told Sam that's she's ready to sell Sansome Springs.

Reckons she's got lodgings here in Worcester and only come forward when she thought Eliza needed help.

It's a wicked trick to pull. Everybody knows that Eliza never got over him going and she wants so badly to hear about him now. Just as she'd found her feet too.

I'll see how she goes on, before I step in but in the meantime, I shall have to get out and talk to that Ana. I never took to her, but she's the one to ask if there's something dirty to be dug up.

CHAPTER FIFTY

'What is it about Sam that worries you?' Ana asked. 'I can tell there's been a change, what has he done?'

Eliza sighed. She depended on her regular chats with Ana, who was more open minded than Alice and didn't care a hoot for the opinion of others.

'It's not what he's done, more what he thinks. He was against me installing a family to manage the mother and baby home and he believes the women who go there should pay for their care.'

'Typical. Strutting around town in his fancy suits made by some poor bugger who can't afford to feed their kids unless they wreck their eyes sewing all night. Greedy bastard.'

Eliza choked on her coffee. 'Hasty, and harsh.'

Ana disagreed. 'That one statement shows you his true colours. He's so grasping he can't bear to see anyone get something for nothing even if it's not him giving it.'

Eliza sipped thoughtfully, she'd been saddened at Sam's disapproval when she'd insisted that the mother and baby home stop charging fees. They'd had a debate about it and she'd realised he wasn't the man she'd thought he was.

She'd tried to dismiss his apparent lack of respect for Ruby as her misunderstanding. But the way he'd spoken about girls who found themselves in trouble told her things about him that she couldn't live with.

'He thinks he knows best, and he'll argue with me, but with no real passion, as though he doesn't really care. I'd thought we were friends, but I don't know anything about what he truly feels.'

'A couple of odd things recently made me wonder. I mentioned that I felt ready to sell Sansome Springs. It's taken me a long time to decide, I've been cautious because it was so important to Ruby and I wanted to do the right thing. Anyway, I finally made up my mind and I told him. He didn't pass comment but a few days ago a woman called at the house.

'She introduced herself as my stepmother and informed me that she owns a quarter share in Sansome Springs. I was shocked, and frightened. I invited her and let her talk, thinking I might get to the bottom of what she's up to.

'She might be telling the truth, she said the papers are lodged with her lawyer, but she'd hoped that as family we would deal amicably. If I doubted her, she said she could prove it.'

Ana raise her eyebrows but kept silent.

'I'm sure she's lying. We'd have known about her, wouldn't we? And why would she turn up now?'

She clenched her fists in frustration. 'She's a dreadful woman and I won't give her anything without a fight.'

'Yes, I think you should be very careful indeed. I know you're a clever girl but, slow down and keep your own counsel for a while would be my advice. You said a couple of things?'

'Yes, he said someone had approached him with an offer to rent a particular building of mine. I don't own it though, and when I told him so, I saw a flash of anger in his eyes. He covered it, but it worried me.'

'You're right to be wary.'

Something in Ana's mild tone alerted Eliza. 'Do you know something I don't?' She asked.

Ana nodded slowly. 'I think I probably do, if you're ready to hear it. But you'll need the whole story and I wonder if you're ready for it?' She looked at Eliza quizzically.

'Go on.'

'Very well, what does Sam say about that patch of land at Bevere?'

Eliza shook her head. 'I'm not even sure it's mine, the document is unclear. I've never mentioned it. It's one of those things I've put by until later.'

'Good. I think it's time you visited Bevere for yourself.'

CHAPTER FIFTY-ONE

Bevere Island was a small parcel of land, unloved and disrespected, situated inconveniently in the middle of the tempestuous Severn, subject to flooding and being no use to man or beast.

Eliza watched as the ferry, the only access to the island, glided in to bump up against the dock. She held her tongue. Ana had promised to explain everything once they were on the island.

The ferryman jumped off and indicated with his head that they were free to climb aboard. As they did so, a man came out from the inn and brought him a brimming jug of ale.

'He'll drink that on the way to the island, turn around, come back here for another. He'll keep going until he falls asleep, or overboard.'

Once on the island they followed a path that twisted through the overgrowth and headily slightly uphill. They came to a clearing and Eliza gasped as she set eyes on an extraordinary long low building, set upon stilts and completely hidden be the screen of trees that circled it.

She climbed the ten steps up to the front door and entered a world of luxury. The polished floorboards glowed and were topped by the richest Turkish rugs upon which sat intricately carved pieces of furniture. Inviting chairs and day couches were scattered at random points throughout.

There were ornate wooden shutters over all the windows. Lamps glowed here and there, but still there were shadowy corners about the place. Just above head height was a gallery that circled the ballroom, this too contained comfortable chairs and gentle lighting.

The staff she saw moving soundlessly about were male and looked to be in prime condition. No ancient retainers took up space here.

'Welcome to La Milagra.' Ana swept her arm out in a gesture of pride. 'We're closed three days a week for cleaning and stocking up and such and I thought it was best for you to come over without customers milling about the place. There's a great deal I can do to help you from here if you're willing to let me.'

Eliza drank in the sumptuous furnishings, she ran her fingers across a deep red silk drape and saw the glow from the nearby lamp reflected in it. 'Is this where you work at night?'

Ana nodded and Eliza replayed in her mind what she knew and what she'd wondered. Things she'd absorbed as a child and then forgotten, things she'd been confused by. 'Tell me what's going on Ana?'

Ana smiled at her. 'Nothing that need worry you, but a great deal to help. Come, let's be comfortable.' She turned and led the way down a short passage and into a small comfortable parlour where she indicated they should sit.

'I can see you're confused and you won't relax until I tell you more. I've told you my mother was a close friend of Ruby's. They met in London years ago and became firm friends. Ruby was with my Ma the first time she saw Vauxhall and that's what started her on the Sansome Springs plan.

'They helped each other out many times over the years. Ma turned to Ruby when she lost the inn and together they built this place. I owe a huge debt to Ruby and it's possible that I can help you now.'

Eliza looked confused.

'Let me explain. This is a club for wealthy gentlemen. We provide everything, food, drink, entertainment, gambling, there is nothing we can't supply.' She looked at Eliza. 'You understand what I'm telling you?'

'Of course.'

'My girls are exceptionally well trained and are completely loyal, discretion is vital, and I trust them all. Everything they see and hear is reported to me, but it goes no further. Our gentlemen can rest easy, we've never betrayed a member yet, but all the information we've gleaned is stored away.

'I know who is doing what in the city, I know who has plans, who has expectations, and who has worries, and very often I know what they intend to do about it.

'And you've heard something connected to me?'

'I've never intended to betray my clients, I may have used information I've overheard for my own gain, but I've never repeated anything to another soul. I've never even considered it, until now.'

CHAPTER FIFTY-TWO

'My girls know not to tattle, anything out of the ordinary they bring to me. It's how I know so much about our city. Two young fellows were having a bit of falling about a girl with no sense and more money than she knew what to do with. They were deciding who had the better chance of marrying her, and who'd have her sister.'

Seeing Eliza's look of shock made Ana smile. 'That's not an entirely unusual subject for young men to be preoccupied with, sometimes it's drink and sometimes it's showing off but it's rarely sinister.'

Eliza cleared her throat. 'You're talking about my cousins, and they were talking about me?'

'When I first heard, I wasn't certain, but I wondered. I made it my business to watch out for them and I shadowed them. Sam has the upper hand, no doubt about that, but they want what you've got.'

'What shall I do?' Eliza's eyes clouded over, she clearly didn't want an answer yet.

Ana rang a tiny bell that sat on the table and a man came out bearing a tea tray and a bottle of spirit. Ana filled a cup - half and half - and pushed it into Eliza's hands. "Drink it.'

Eliza gulped, then gasped.

'I'd advise you to take your time, mull things over and compare what I've told you with what you know and don't forget, them fooling you is their shame not yours. What you do about it, that's what will matter.'

Eliza felt betrayed and foolish. They'd come home with their fancy clothes and pretty manners and she'd been as witless as Georgie. Blinded by false glamour.

'I'm such a fool.'

Ana grasped her chin and looked her in the eye. 'No! You were almost tricked, that makes them cruel but is no reflection on you. Turn your anger outwards to them, not inside you.'

She welcomed the burn of anger that swept away her lingering self-pity. How could those two, who she'd known since childhood plot to rob her, their own family? And how could she punish them?

Ana raised her hands and stepped back. 'You'll know what to do when your mind is straight. That's partly why I brought you here to tell you. I wanted you to understand how I came by the information I have, and I wanted to be certain we weren't overheard. You can talk and ponder out here and no-one will be any wiser.

'Ruby told me once, when you know something that the others fellow thinks you don't know, you've got the upper hand. Take heart, they haven't got away with it.'

Eliza tapped her lips with her fingers. 'That's right, they don't know their nasty secret has been exposed.'

CHAPTER FIFTY-THREE

She accepted Ana's invitation to have a tour of La Milagra. Peeking into the private chambers and the hidden nooks that enable the girls to eavesdrop in comfort, marvelling at the luxurious dining area and openly envying the glittering chandelier, all took time.

Time for this new information to sink in and time for her anger to lower to a simmer.

She smiled sadly at Ana. 'Thank you for telling me.'

Ana squeezed her hand before hugging her. 'I wish it hadn't happened, but you'll come good. Keep it to yourself and think long and hard until you're ready.'

Eliza barely noticed the journey back and had to make haste to jump off the ferry as it came alongside beside Pitchcroft. Ana had advised her to go home, but she had always found peace in walking and she wanted to have a calm mind before getting home.

She let the events of the past play through her mind and the mistakes she'd made since Ruby had died. Her doomed relationship with Peter had been nothing more than laziness on both their parts, he bore no more blame than she did.

Sam was different, he'd set out to charm her and found her easily won, sickeningly so. With the benefit of a little experience and a whole bundle of knowledge, she realised how well he'd manipulated her. He was clever and cold. A man who'd stop at nothing to get what he wanted. She counted herself fortunate to have discovered what he wanted before he'd been able to take it.

But it was Freddy's betrayal that had knocked her so badly. She was horrified that she'd been so wrong about him. She'd felt a real connection between them. But she didn't doubt Ana's evidence, he was in cahoots with Sam.

She forced herself to keep mulling everything over, needing to get used to their betrayal and the pain it was causing her. She wanted to scream out her bitter disappointment to his face but holding back and waiting would help her in the long run. But God, it hurt.

She walked until her feet throbbed, but she'd shed no more tears and was feeling thankful for the friend who'd been able to prevent her from making a catastrophic error.

A man yelled out, cursing her for a fool. She looked up and was startled to find herself in danger of being mown down by a wagon leaving Worcester bridge.

Seeing she was so close to St Johns, she decided to carry on and visit Uncle Hugh who was delighted to see her and too polite to remark on her appearance.

'My dear girl, what a lovely surprise, come in do.'

'I need some help Uncle Hugh and you made me promise to come to you if I feared I was out of my depth.'

'And I'm thrilled that you have, sit down and tell me what's on your mind?'

'Since I removed our business from Givens I'd struggled to make head or tail of our finances.'

'Why you didn't come to me in the beginning…'

'Please Uncle Hugh.'

'Yes, yes. Go on.'

'Sam came along at the right time, Aunt Ellie wanted me talk to him, and I appreciated the help. He's offered me some advice, but before I act, I wondered what you thought of him? We're family and I don't any awkwardness between any of us but, confidentially, do you have an opinion on his business abilities?'

Hugh placed his hands on his knees and tapped his fingers, clearly gathering his words.

'Confidentially you say?' He held his gaze on Eliza until she nodded.

'As a legal man there's no doubt he worked harder and learned a lot more than Freddy did so his abilities in that arena are good. He's clever and quick witted. When it comes to business, he has no experience, so I imagine your judgement is as solid as his.'

'You don't like him?'

Hugh agreed. 'Sadly, I don't, and I wouldn't trust him. He's sly and I don't believe he has an honourable bone in his body. He's been a bad influence for my son, although that's not entirely his fault.

'I wish I could have nothing more to do with him, but that would hurt Ellie, who is the silliest woman I know, but is family, as you say.'

Eliza cleared her throat. 'Thank you for being honest, I won't repeat a word. One more question?'

'Of course.'

'The Daventor school building? Why has it been left it empty and unused?'

He sat upright, a frown across his face. 'How odd that you should ask me that.'

'Sam said something that made me wonder, is it mine?'

'Oh yes, most certainly. Freddy approached me, only last week, he and Sam had some ridiculous idea of converting it to a grand arcade, shops and salons and the like. I don't think his heart was in it, to be honest. He didn't look too worried when I told him the building wasn't mine to give.

'I was sure the deeds were amongst the papers I gave you but possibly not. I'll dig them out, they've always been in my possession.'

Seeing Eliza's confusion, he explained.

'There's no question about the ownership. Ruby wanted to provide an education for you girls, but she couldn't find a quality school nearby that would take you and she was determined not to send you away.

'She decided - and bullied me into agreeing - that we would build a school. We'd start with our own offspring, you three, my crowd and Ellie's boys. We'd build it up to a point where we could offer a few free places to those in need.

'She'd always resented not having an education and was determined to do better for others. She didn't have the best reputation though.'

Eliza felt his eyes on her and her cheeks flamed but she looked at him proudly. 'I've heard the stories. To us she was a saviour. I loved her, and I respected her.'

'As do I. But she knew that she could never be associated in any way with such an undertaking. She funded the entire thing and I was the face of the school.

'We enjoyed a good few years, but running a school is a massive undertaking and, after a run of bad luck, and one tragic incident, we had no choice but to close our doors.

Eliza still had questions. 'The HH carved in the stones above the gateway, everyone assumes it's your family initials.'

He sighed and shook his head. 'It was a joke. We allowed it to be thought it stood for Henry and Hugh, but it didn't. It was for the Harlot's Horde.'

'That's ugly!'

'It had meaning to her. She'd been called some wicked things all her life and brushed it off. When she started work on Sansome Springs, it was dubbed the harlot's garden by the folks who watched and waited to see her fail. I have to say, she gloried in the title. She was never ashamed or apologetic you see, so what they called her was almost irrelevant.'

He laughed. 'Until she achieved success, of course. Then she delighted in rubbing peoples noses in their past judgements of her. She gave the city the school and didn't need or want thanks, but she couldn't resist putting her mark on it.'

'She turned something pretty unpleasant into that mother and baby home which helped countless women and I'll wager never earned her a penny. The thing about Ruby was, she liked herself, so the opinion of others mattered not one jot.'

'I wish I'd had longer with her, I have so many questions and now it's too late.'

He wrapped her in a hug. 'Never doubt that she loved you dearly and did her best for you. She shaped you, I can see her in you, and that makes me a lucky man. Don't waste your time with regrets. She'd expect you to forge ahead and make something wonderful with your life, as she did.'

She squeezed him back and smiled. 'I'm going to stop running the library, it bores me to be honest. I'm sure someone will be glad of the chance to take it over. I'm going to take control of what she left behind and make it mine.

CHAPTER FIFTY-FOUR

MARY

Oh ho, looks to me like something's happened to break up the cosy twosome.

She's walking about with a closed face and not even Georgie's asking her what's up.

The last few times Sam's called she was out, and the look on his face was a picture. The first time he was surprised, the next he was downright bloody angry if you ask me.

The third time he called, Georgie insisted he be shown in and she entertained him herself. He left with a bit more bounce in his step than he came in with, I can tell you that for nothing.

I smell trouble, he's as sharp as they come and, with the best will in the world, Georgie's a drip.

But then, if he's as mucky as his Pa, he won't care about that, not if he's looking for a trough to rob. And according to Ana, he's every inch his Pa. Not that she'll say more than that.

Eliza's just like a cat on coals, snapping and snarling at all of us. Put me in mind of Ruby when she was spoiling for a fight.

She's having a tough time of it, but every time something hits her, I see her get stronger. And let's be honest, we all have a certain amount of muck to shovel in our lives, this is Eliza's time.

I'll keep an eye on her, she'll be right now the truth is out, no doubt about that.

CHAPTER FIFTY-FIVE

Eliza took Ana's advice to heart and did her best to keep her enemies close.

Sam saw though her though. He'd pestered and questioned her at every turn, his frustration clear. She assured him all was well and there was little he could do, but she knew time was running out.

Knowing how close she'd come to making a terrible error sickened her. She'd been attracted to him and that, combined with her delight at finding someone to share her burden had almost blinded her. What upset her most was the extent of her own gullibility, that had been a hard lesson to learn.

The woman posing as her step-mama was a fake, but she didn't yet know who she really was, and she didn't want to act until she was sure. She smiled and listened but signed nothing.

An outright falling out now would not serve her well so she did all she could to ease his concerns and was quick to assure him that she was taking some thinking time and had made no firm plans that he should know about, but it was hard.

To smile, to pour tea, and to make light conversation was difficult but the last thing she wanted was a rift with Aunt Ellie, hadn't her family lost enough as it was? But he'd infuriated her, and she would punish him somehow.

Her feelings for Freddy were different. Their relationship was not business oriented and she'd found it easier to avoid him without it seeming obvious. He'd attended their recent supper and made a bee line for her.

She was taken aback to see what seemed to be honest hurt in his eyes when she was coolly polite.

She reminded herself that the two men had been best friends for twenty years, how could they not be cut from the same cloth? It hurt her badly to know that he was partner with a cheating bully and she lost all confidence in her judgement when it came to men.

She decided she'd been on the right path before she met those two cheats, she was better off alone. Men, and interfering friends, had proved to be more trouble than they were worth.

At breakfast she announced that there'd be no more suppers. 'You have enough admirers to start a war Georgie, and I have too much work to do to be bothered with the nonsense.'

She turned to fix her eyes on her sister. 'If Aunt Ellie has anything to say about that, then be good enough to tell her, from me, that she's welcome to have as many suppers as she'd like in her own home.'

Arthur, Georgie and Emily sat in silence, shocked at her vehemence.

'Good. We've agreed on something.' She said, leaving the room.

CHAPTER FIFTY-SIX

Eliza's stomach growled, and she tossed a glance of apology Ana's way. 'I hadn't realised how late it was, come home and eat with us?'

Ana nodded casually. Although Eliza was rarely at the library the two managed to meet twice a week and Ana knew as much about the Morgan's business as Eliza did.

Ana proved a satisfactory confidante, always practical with a large dose of common sense and a refusal to indulge in sentiment. She enjoyed sharing her wisdom, and happily dished out snippets of gossip she thought might be relevant. It was not unusual for the afternoon walk to extend into dinner and on through the evening.

Ana nodded. 'I hope Mary's cooked a horse, my belly thinks my throat's been cut.'

'Sorry, I've kept us out much longer than I should have.'

'Don't worry, it's exciting. I'm proud to see you taking charge.'

They stepped into the house and Eliza sniffed the air. 'Smells more like lamb than horse. Sit down, I'll go and tell Mary we're home.'

She inhaled deeply as she entered the kitchen. 'That smells good. Have Georgie and Emily eaten?'

Mary shrugged. 'I haven't seen them, I thought they were with you.'

'No, they went to visit Caroline, but they should be back by now.' Eliza felt a twist of concern in her stomach.

'Georgie knows Emily hates the dark, it would be unusual for her to stay out so late. I'll go and check upstairs, they might be up there. If not, I'll run to Caroline's and fetch them.'

She ran up the stairs knowing they weren't there, it was impossible for them to be awake and silent. She picked up the note that had been left in the centre of her dresser and screamed as she ran down the stairs.

Ana and Mary came running and she waved the note at them. 'She's eloped with Sam and taken Emily with her.' She threw the note down. 'Mary, run and fetch Aunt Ellie, and don't take any of her nonsense. She bears some responsibility for this.'

'Ana...'

Ana was already heading for the door. 'I'll go to their office. If Sam's away, then Freddy will be there. I'll drag him here if I have to.'

'And don't worry about Ellie giving me nonsense, I know her of old.' Mary muttered as she ran out.

With Mary and Ana gone there was nothing to prevent Eliza cursing her selfish sister. She'd always known Georgie couldn't see the right option if it stubbed her on the toe, but to have involved Emily was unforgiveable.

Aunt Ellie, propelled by a grim-faced Mary, stumbled over the doorstep.

'Don't be too upset Eliza, I know you're shocked but...' She paused for breath. 'Mary's not making sense, kidnap, indeed!' She sucked in air. 'I ran all the way here.'

'Only 'cos I had the toe of my boot up your arse.'

'So rude!' Ellie wailed.

'Read this then tell me what you know.' Eliza impatiently waved the scrap of paper in her aunt's face.

Aunt Ellie snatched at the paper and used it to fan herself dramatically.

'You'd better tell me what you know Ellie. I've sent for Freddy and we shall go after them, but I should like to be prepared.'

Ellie put her hand across her mouth. 'They have become fond of one another and I know that you disapproved of them, which was foolish of you my dear. Love can't be denied.'

'Oh, for goodness sake Ellie, they're not in love.' Eliza snapped angrily. 'Sam is incapable of loving anyone but himself, as you know very well. As for Georgie, she'll do anything to place herself at the centre of a drama. I blame you, and your romantic notions for encouraging her. I'm sure Sam has a reason for doing this and I'm equally sure it has nothing to do with love.'

A steely glance quashed Ellies protests. 'If Georgie is prepared to throw away her good name, that is one thing, but to involve Emily is another thing altogether. It *is* kidnapping, and I will have the law on him before morning. Now, where might they have gone?'

Ellie clutched her chest and it was clear that this was a shock to her. 'They've taken Emily, but why? How reckless of them…'

'Stop wittering and think, where could they have gone?' Eliza said sharply.

They all turned as the front door swung open and Freddy stood there. He stepped in and grasped Eliza's hand. 'Tell me what's happened, I'll help.'

Despite everything, Eliza felt relief at the sight of him. She passed him Georgie's note.

'They've run away, eloped according to Georgie. Which is stupid enough, but far worse, they've taken Emily with them.'

He cursed and sighed deeply before turning to Ellie who was quietly sobbing. 'You have no idea where they might have gone and you're certain they are not hiding somewhere nearby?'

Ellie could manage no more than a moan. He dismissed her with a toss of his head and addressed Eliza. 'Wrap up warmly. I'll hire a chaise from the Star. I have an idea.'

Eliza, glad of something to do, ran upstairs and loaded herself up with warm clothing, for herself and her sisters, doubting Georgie would have done anything so practical.

Just hours before, she'd been laughing with Ana as they plotted ever more outrageous acts of revenge on her disloyal cousins. All she wanted now was to have her sisters' safely home.

Mary thrust a hefty basket into her arms as she climbed aboard the buggy, beside Freddy. 'You haven't eaten a bite, dip into that as you go.'

Freddy clipped the reigns and she was jolted back on the bench seat.

'We knew a chap at university, a minister's son who was filling in time before he found a church of his own. He and Sam had some wild times, thick as thieves they were. Sam always had a hold on him. He's out in Cheltenham now and I imagine if Sam has a hasty marriage on his mind that's where he'll head.'

Eliza gripped the handrail, torn between concern for Emily and her desire to learn more about Sam, Freddy and their odd relationship.

'Does Sam have marriage on his mind though, or is this more trickery?'

'Eliza.' Freddy began, then shook his head. 'I know what Sam chooses to tell me and no more. I can promise you I know nothing about this escapade, I would never have gone along with such a ridiculous enterprise.'

'And yet you're closely involved in so many of his other enterprises'

'I can tell you've uncovered something, but I need to pay attention to the track if we're to stand any chance of catching them safely. If I promise I'll tell you everything when we get them home, can you wait?'

He glanced at her and then back at the track, they moved at a rapid pace and he could not risk losing control of the horses. The biting wind cut across her face, but Eliza barely noticed. She scanned the track in front and the open ground to the sides, her mind racing.

She wanted to trust him, to lean on him, and all she really cared about was the safety of her troublesome sisters.

CHAPTER FIFTY-SEVEN

Freddy reached across and gave her hand a reassuring squeeze, as though he knew what she was thinking, but would not fall into false reassurance.

'How long have they been gone?'

She shrugged and twisted her hands together. 'I'm not sure, probably two hours. I hadn't noticed. I was so…'

'Now's not the time to blame yourself. Tell me what happened.'

'Georgie was bored, and I was keen to get out for a walk. When she said she wanted to visit her friend I was pleased. She normally visits for an hour and comes home. I didn't worry as Emily only panics as darkness falls, you see.'

'Mmmh. Going on that, they might be an hour in front of us, we'll catch up with them, I'm sure.'

'That's if they've gone this way.' She said as she dashed tears from her cheeks. Her head slumped, and she groaned, imagining Emily's fear of the dark.

'Pointless thing to say!' He said briskly. 'Don't start that foolish nonsense now, this is our best guess and we're following it. Do you have a better idea?'

His sharp tone did the trick. 'Sorry, I was being absurd. I appreciate you helping.'

'I care for my cousins, you especially.' He said.

They plunged on through the rapidly darkening night. Eliza found an apple in the basket, she took a bite and then tossed it away.

A scream rang out, some distance ahead, an unearthly bellow of agony.

'That was pretty close.' Freddy reigned in the horses.

'You keep your eyes on that side, I'll watch this one.'

A few yards on light flared nearby, as someone from a nearby cottage came out to investigate.

'What's the noise about, what's happened?' Freddy shouted.

'I reckon a carriage overturned, some damn fool was going too fast, there's a wicked bend in the track here, it's a stream you see. Follow me, I can guess where they've landed.'

Freddy followed until they could see the carriage on its side at the edge of a twisting waterway. The ungodly screaming came from one of the horses who was frantically kicking to escape.

Freddy took control, directing the first cottager to deal with the animal while his sons were brought closer to illuminate the interior of the carriage, leaving them in no doubt that they had found their quarry.

'Emily! Georgie! I'm here.' Eliza called as she fumbled uselessly to open the carriage door. The sheer weight of it as it lay on its side was too great for her.

Freddy grasped her by the shoulders and eased her away. 'Step back. I need room and light to work.'

A shot rang out and the horse fell silent.

A pool of flickering light helped them see the twins bundled together, Georgie sobbing, Emily motionless.

'I'm sorry Eliza.' Georgie reached one hand up towards them.

'Are you hurt?' Freddy barked at her.

'No, no I don't think so.'

'Then reach up and give me your arm, I'll need to get you out of the way so that I can lift Emily out.'

She wailed at the mention of her twin and he snapped. 'That's not helping anything. Reach up as far as you can and take my hand, I'll pull you out. Come on.

Freddy hauled her up as far as he could manage, allowing the cottager to grasp her around the waist and dump her, unceremoniously on the side of the track, for Eliza to deal with.

'The other one's a bit delicate,' Freddy explained to his unknown helper. 'We'll have to go easy with her.' The man nodded.

'Emily, can you reach out for my hand?' He called gently but she ignored him.

It was then that Sam, who had been crushed beneath Georgie, groaned and blinked in the light. 'What the…Freddy is that you?'

'Wake up Sam. You've had an accident and I need your help to get Emily out. Come on man, wake up.'

Sam raised his head and looked for a moment as though he was going to pass out again, he was deathly pale and clearly unsteady, but Freddy pulled him back.

'Come on man, get a hold of yourself. I can't get in there, you'll have to help us lift her, I think she's hurt.'

'I can't move my legs.'

'Use your arms then! We need to get her out. This is all your doing, so get a hold of yourself.'

Sam nodded and turned to Emily as Freddy watched nervously. Thus far Emily had remained still and silent, but Freddy knew her well enough to know that she could panic at any second and then she'd be impossible to manage.

'Be ready, I'll lift her as high as I'm able. You'll need to take the weight.'

'Just get on with it!' Freddy lay flat along the side of the carriage and lowered his head and shoulder as the others held the torch aloft.

Eliza watched his back twist as he took the weight of Emily and then slowly wriggled himself back until the other man could grasp Emily around her waist and lower her to the ground.

Eliza dropped to her knees. 'Oh, dear God I think she's…'

The cottager stepped forward and pulled her away. 'Let me get her into the light Miss.'

He and Freddy lifted her between them, exposing the mat of blood-soaked hair.

Georgie ran forwards and tried to pull her from their arms, screaming when they pushed her away. Eliza slapped her so hard her head snapped back, shocking her into silence.

Eliza turned away from her.

She wanted to lash out at Georgie for her selfish recklessness.

She wanted to grab the old man's gun and shoot Sam.

She wanted Emily to stop playing this awful trick on her. Poor Emily couldn't be dead, she could not be dead.

It was her job to keep the twins from killing each other. Wasn't that the last thing Papa asked her to do?

CHAPTER FIFTY-EIGHT

MARY

Didn't I always say Sam Pargeter was trouble?

This last business was worse than anything I expected though. Poor Emily is dead and buried and the horror of it has almost killed Eliza.

It sticks in my craw to admit that it's Freddy that's getting us through. I never saw any good in him, I knew his father was a decent man, but I thought Freddy was a fool and bone idle. One of them, too rich and handsome for their own good, types.

I was wrong, he's here every blessed day and not causing any extra work. He takes her a tray of tea up and sits and reads the paper to her.

She's not uttered a word since we said goodbye to Emily, but still he comes and talks to her.

He stayed with her the night Emily died and he stuck by her side as she talked to the doctor and then the magistrate.

It was him that stopped Eliza from killing Georgie when she screamed and tried to climb onto the wagon with poor dead Emily. The slap Eliza gave her shocked them both. Freddy stepped forward and wrapped an arm around each one of them and turned them away from the wagon, so they couldn't watch Emily being driven off.

Freddy took charge of the magistrate's man and dealt with everything else.

This is the saddest house in Worcester and God only knows what's to become of us.

CHAPTER FIFTY-NINE

As far as Eliza was concerned the list of Sam's crimes merged into one seething mess, she was consumed with hatred. She needed him to suffer and until he did she wouldn't rest. She sat in her chair and plotted, day after day.

The house was never free of visitors, each one bearing advice on what she should do to move on, get a fresh start and get over it.

She screamed and threw the tea tray at Aunt Ellie when she said those stupid words. As Ellie wailed and ran to the door Eliza's voice followed her.

'If you honestly think the needless death of my innocent sister, caused by your son, is something I'll ever *get over* then I have nothing to say to you.'

Alice, glowing with personal happiness, but trying to subdue it, brought gifts and kisses. She urged Eliza to go to church, suggesting maybe she'd find peace there. Eliza told her to get out too.

Ana came, all piss and vinegar, and begged to be allowed to wreak her own brand of revenge on Sam, describing in glorious detail what she'd get one of her girls to do to him if only Eliza would say the word.

Uncle Hugh told her she needed to get back to work. He urged her to think of the women out at the home and their dependence on her good management. She lied when she agreed with him.

And every day there was Freddy, and not once did he tell her what she should do.

Eliza sat with a piece of sewing on her lap that had not felt the prick of a needle since the day of the accident. It was something to keep her eyes on, she couldn't bear to see people.

The reminders of Emily where everywhere and she never stopped seeing her. Smiling shyly, her childlike eyes watching Georgie with complete trust. Giggling happily when it was just the three of them and she knew she was safe. Shining with innocence and trust. Every memory broke her heart a little more.

It was safer to fix her eyes on the sewing and keep her mind blank.

The door behind her opened, but she didn't bother to look up, it didn't matter who it might be. People came and commiserated daily but only to make themselves feel better, to be seen doing the right thing. She had no interest in playing those games.

When a hand fell on her shoulder she knew it was her sister, no-one else dared touch her. She shrugged the hand away and Georgie moved to sit quietly in a chair some distance away from her sister.

'What on earth were you thinking?'

Eliza's voice was gravelly from disuse and Georgie stiffened with surprise. Eliza hadn't spoken to her for so long.

"You want to talk about it?'

'I want to understand.'

Georgie, unsettled at this turn in events, became defensive. 'You shouldn't have laughed at me.'

Eliza's hand twitched, she hated Georgie as much as she loved her. She'd managed to drag her twin to her death and still she wanted a reason to blame Eliza.

'Nothing you did was my fault. You took Emily away from the safety of home and risked her life for reasons of your own. What was it that you wanted that was worth more than her life?'

Georgie hung her head.

'I thought I knew the extent of your stupidity, but I never imagined that you'd take a risk with Emily. What could have possessed you?'

Georgie's face filled with colour and she twisted her hands in her lap. 'You won't understand, you never listen to me for long enough to understand.'

'I'm here now and I'm going nowhere so why don't you give it a try?'

'I'd wanted to talk to you for such a long time. To tell you how sorry I was for being difficult and to see if I could help you. I saw how excited you were with your business and I thought you might enjoy talking to me. But you were too busy, always too busy and I stopped trying.'

'I don't remember you ever trying to talk to me.' Eliza shook her head.

'I wanted to know what was going on. One minute you were all involved with Sam, meeting and chatting all the time, then you were never at home for him. He called once or twice, hoping to find you and I wanted to know what had changed so I invited him in. We talked about you and your moods.'

'You'd shut everyone out and we wondered why. He was afraid you might be taking bad advice, but he could never get to talk to you. I tried to find out what you were doing, but you wouldn't even tell me.

'We became friends then.' She shrugged. 'We shut you out, as you'd shut us out.'

Eliza kept her head down, emotionless.

'I told him how I'd always hoped I'd grow up to marry Freddy and how childish I felt when he came home, and I saw how ordinary he was. He was kind and he understood.'

'What happened that night?'

Georgie stood up and walked across the room, she glanced briefly in the mirror and then smiled sadly at her sister.

'I wanted to be with Sam, but I thought you'd try to prevent me if I told you. You say *no Georgie* without listening to the question, even though it's not your decision to make.

'We realised that if we were to be together we had to do it and confess afterwards. I convinced him that we should run away and come back as a married couple. It was so thrilling. The most exciting thing that has ever happened to me and I couldn't wait to go, once we'd agreed.'

Eliza shook her head. 'But, why take Emily?'

'She saw me getting ready and realised that I was leaving.' Georgie sniffed and wiped her eyes. 'She cried and begged to come with me.'

Georgie buried her face in her hands and cried as though she'd never stop.

'I couldn't leave her behind, I loved her too much to leave her crying. And now I've lost both of you.

She clapped her hands across her mouth. 'I hope you can forgive me one day, but it doesn't really matter because I'll never forgive myself.'

'Oh Georgie.' Eliza whispered.

CHAPTER SIXTY

As the weeks passed Eliza started to take a daily walk, sometimes alone and sometimes with one or another of her friends. She decided when and she decided who, reasoning that she'd look after her own self and they could join in or bugger off.

Ana didn't quite mask her shock when she called to find Eliza up and dressed in walking clothes. 'You're going out?'

'I thought a walk, join me?'

'I'd like to say you're looking better, but I've never lied to you and I don't see that I should start now. Dear God, you're all bones.'

Eliza smiled at the honesty she had come to expect from her friend. 'Good thing I don't keep you around for flattery.'

Ana let out a laugh. 'What do you keep me around for?'

'I can be myself with you. You don't fuss, you don't let me get away with being rude, you don't tell me it'll get better, you listen to me, and you make me laugh, even when I don't want to.'

'No, I won't fuss, but, when did you last eat a proper meal?'

'I've got no appetite, Mary cooks her heart out but…'

Ana flapped her hands in dismissal. 'I don't really care, you'll eat when you're ready. I just felt it was my duty, as your friend, to ask.'

They walked in silence, enjoying the day. Ana thankful to see Eliza looking better, not good, but better.

She'd leave it to Mary and the family to see that she didn't lose any more weight. Privately Ana thought the sooner she got back to work the better she'd be, but she was wise enough to keep that opinion to herself.

'What news of Georgie?'

Eliza tugged Ana's arm and they headed in the direction of Sansome Springs, the first time in a year at least.

'The silly cat is adamant that once this year ends she and Sam will marry. Ellie supports them, and Hugh says that I should let them get on with it, and I've decided I shall. It might be the best thing all round. I dearly want Sam's suffering to continue, and I can't imagine anything worse than having Georgie as a nurse.'

'He still needs nursing?'

Eliza shrugged, then nodded. 'I won't listen to talk of him, but I've heard her and Ellie twittering. It seems that losing his leg almost caused him a breakdown. You know how vain he was.'

'His peacock strutting days are over then.'

'That they are, and he's got fat, because according to Ellie he won't do anything for himself. He sits in a chair like the king and has them all running around after him. She's at her wits end. I think that's partly why she's encouraging Georgie, it's someone to share her load.'

Ana looked at her in disbelief. 'Georgie wouldn't run around after him like that?'

'Perhaps, for a time. She's not used to accepting guilt and is desperate to feel better about herself. I won't let her use me that way, so I think Sam will be the recipient.

'I think… I think they might be good for each other. And I also think it's time I stopped worrying about her.'

Ana said nothing.

'Well, don't you have anything to say?' Eliza demanded.

'Only you know how you feel and what you're ready for. If you're looking to me for guidance or encouragement you're wasting a good walk. I'm your friend, but I won't do your thinking for you.'

'Thank heavens for that, I can think perfectly well for myself. In fact, I may not stop doing now I've started.'

Ana laughed. 'I always knew that. You needed to trust yourself, that's all. What have you been plotting?'

'Not plotting, reflecting. All the nonsense that I was worried about, the time I spent arguing with Sam. It was because I wanted him to approve of me even as I disapproved of him.'

'That's normal. We meet someone, there's something that attracts us to them, so we ignore the bits we don't like, make allowances. That's what makes you a woman. But when you saw he was wrong you argued with him and did what you knew was right, that's what makes you special. Forgive yourself for wanting to impress him but praise yourself for seeing through him.'

Eliza nodded, but remained serious. 'I need to get back to work. I have to fill my mind with…other things.'

'Hmm.'

'I've looked at a couple of reports and…' She swallowed, unable to speak.

Ana waited.

'Some of the things I argued with Sam about have turned out exceptionally well. I haven't paid attention to anything for months, yet everything has settled. I thought I was making the right choices, now I have proof.

'This has been the worst year of my life, but I feel a deep sense of satisfaction, knowing I've made some good decisions.

'Giving the Barker's control of the mother and baby home was the turning point. It does pays for itself, as it always has. Proof that I can manage my business, and I can deal with men. The ones that don't like it are the ones I enjoy the most.

Ana laughed. 'I suggest you keep that little gem quiet.'

'I don't care what anyone thinks. I'm going to do what Ruby trained me to do as well as I can.'

They continued through Sansome Springs in silence.

'Can I ask you something?' Eliza asked.

Ana nodded.

'Why have you never married?'

Ana laughed in surprise. 'I don't trust men. Don't misunderstand me, I like them well enough, but all the trouble in my life can be traced back to a man.

'My Ma owned an inn that had been in her family for a hundred years. Her husband, a man she took a good long time to get to know, hung onto it for ten years before he gambled it away. He loved her, and she loved him – love's not enough.

'I'm perfectly happy using them for my own ends. Every man I take something from is paying for what the one before did, and I don't care.'

Ana reached out and touched Eliza's elbow, then waited until her friend looked at her 'You're not like me though, and it's no good trying to be something you're not.'

'No, I don't think I am. But I'm not like Georgie either. I don't quite know where I fit in, I'm not sure what I am like. But don't worry, I've learned my lesson. I'll do what I think is best and ignore all the others, at least then any mistakes I make will be mine and I won't have to blame anyone else. Holding a grudge is as wearing as fending off false admirers. I shudder to think how terribly attracted to Sam I was.'

'And Freddy, was that different?' Ana asked, giving her a quick squeeze. 'Did you really care for him?'

Eliza let out a bitter laugh. 'I was torn between the two of them for a time but yes, Freddy was special. It hurt me more than I can say to know that he was a cheat. I was wounded at his betrayal.

'He stepped in when Emily... you know. He took care of everything and I wouldn't have managed without him. He acted like the man I had been sure he was. He still does. He calls, two and three times every week. He talks to Georgie and then he sits quietly with me. I feel relaxed, safe when he's there.'

'You should talk to him. People are strange, they get things twisted or they step onto the wrong track. It might be helpful to bring it out into the open, let the air blow through it.'

Eliza shrugged and looked away. 'I don't talk to him, hello and goodbye is all he gets. I don't feel ready for more, it doesn't matter what his motives were.'

Ana thought it was a good time to change the subject. 'You're a clever woman and you'll find your own way when you're ready.'

'Yes. I'd already started by giving Jacob and John a third each interest in the newspaper with full control to run it as they wish. They'd earned it.'

'You retained the third portion?'

'No. They'll have control of it, but the intention was for the income from it to go into a fund for Emily.' She sucked in a deep breath and Ana guided her to a shabby wooden bench.

'Take a minute, there's no hurry, a few deep breaths.' Ana held her while she cried.

'Sorry. It catches me unawares. It's not as though I forget, but it's not always at the front on my mind. And then suddenly it is, and it hits me like a fresh blow. Does it ever get better?'

Ana wrapped her in a hug and thought of her own mother, dead for ten years and yet she still caught the blows. 'You learn how to live with it, that's all I can promise.' She whispered.

It was a good half an hour before Eliza picked up the conversation where she'd dropped it.

'The income from Emily's fund will go directly to the birthing home in her name. It will be a modest sum, but I know the Barkers will put it to good use.

'As for all of this.' She waved her arms out to encompass Sansome Springs. 'I've had several offers from people wanting to buy the land and I almost sold it when I was desperate, but that woman turned up and made me think.'

'Yes, the confusion about the shares. How did you sort it all out?'

'Ruby had offered a quarter each, one to Pa, one to Mary, one to Barnabus and she kept the other, years ago. Mary wanted nothing to do with it and handed hers back. When Barnabus decided to go to France, Ruby bought his share back, that's where all her money went.

'Sam hired that woman to play my step-mama, not realising that years ago Pa wrote to Ruby, telling her that everything he had was to be ours. The woman was a fake but if she'd have been real I doubt they'd have got anything.

'The important thing is that his trickery slowed me down, gave me time to re-consider, and I've decided that I'm going to hold on to it. It's a piece of Ruby that I can't let go. Not yet.'

CHAPTER SIXTY-ONE

Ana's advice to talk to Freddy pestered her. She was afraid of losing the security she felt when he visited but she couldn't dismiss his dishonesty and simply let things be.

But if she forced everything out into the open and made him explain himself she might then know too much to ignore. She might have to lose him altogether and that would leave a terrible hole in her life. She stiffened her spine, she had to know the truth and then move on.

'Freddy, we need to talk.' She spoke quickly, not allowing herself to stop the words.

He visibly started, before raising his head from the newspaper. She read confusion, or perhaps it was panic, on his face and she held firm.

He cleared his throat. 'Eliza?'

She told him what she knew of the club at Bevere. 'You were overheard, you and Sam. I have something you both want, and you were plotting to get the *upper hand with that Morgan cat.* His exact words, I believe?'

She watched his reaction, shame, resignation, and back to shame.

'You lied to me and pretended to be what you're not. You let me think you had feelings for me and made a fool of me for your own ends.

'You've been a support these last months but that won't cancel the wrong you tried to do. I'm ready to move forward and I plan to retain what's good for me and get rid of what isn't. I need to decide which you are.'

He set the paper to one side. 'I do owe you an explanation and an apology. I swear, my feelings for you are true and they were from the minute I met you. I'll tell you everything, then you must tell me what I can do to make things right.'

She looked at him with something approaching pity. 'This can't be made right Freddy. Emily is dead, Sam's a cripple, and as for Georgie, well…. The best you can do is help me understand.'

He rubbed his hands over his face and sighed heavily.

CHAPTER SIXTY-TWO

He'd known since the accident that everything would have to come out, he wanted it too. The damage that he and Sam had caused was a weight he could hardly bear, but he did, knowing he had to keep it close until Eliza was ready to hear the story.

'It started when we were at school. I did something terrible, something I'm deeply ashamed of.

'Sam was a witness and he convinced me that my confession would create a scandal that could damage Pa's reputation and might destroy his business.

'I was grateful to him for standing by me. I was too scared to be sensible. I should have admitted what I'd done and dealt with the consequences, but I took his advice and kept quiet and he's held it over me ever since. I fell into the habit of following where he led. I was so ashamed.

'I felt I owed him you see. Going to London to study law? That was his dream, but he wanted a companion, so I persuaded Pa that it was what I wanted, though I hated every minute. I was in so far that I couldn't break away.'

'You're saying he blackmailed you?'

His humiliation burned. 'It wasn't overt, initially. He had this saying though, whenever I wasn't as co-operative as he wanted me to be. *Friends stick together.* I knew what he meant.'

'What could you have done that was bad enough to give him such power over you?'

'It was at school. I've already told you that, sorry. We had a game…' He shook his head in frustration.

'I thought up a monthly challenge. Steal some drink, it didn't matter where from and bring it to the loft at school. Those who brought the most could stay and drink it with me and Sam. It was strictly against the rules, so every boy there tried to impress us. There was always horseplay, just boyish pranks, nothing out of the way. But then Tommy Chambers died.'

She looked at him blankly.

He dropped his head into his hands. 'I don't remember much, I was drunk. There were a few of us all drinking and playing cards and I did something stupid and he fell.'

'No!'

He clenched his hands into fists. 'I'll never forgive myself. I wanted to tell you first, now it's time I told Pa. I can't put it right, but I can clear the air with him and I'll do what he suggests.'

She shook her head impatiently. 'He lied to you, he's evil. You should have spoken out at the time, because then you would have known that you didn't kill Tommy. We knew about your stupid drinking games, we used to sneak out of our room and watch you fooling about.

'Tommy often hid with us. We girls babied him, his father was a brute and we felt sorry for him. He was with us that night, in our childish minds we imagined we were keeping him safe.

'His father came in shouting for him and he panicked. He ran up the ladder and jumped from the window. You were nowhere near it, no-one was.'

He leaned back in the chair, his face grey. 'That was the story the school put out, I remember it well. But Sam said he'd seen what happened and that I should keep quiet.

'You know for a fact that I didn't kill him?' He whispered the question. A strange light in his eyes.

She shook her head. 'You were nowhere near him when he fell. I promise.'

'Sam made the whole thing up? And then held it over me for ten years? I can't…'

'He's evil.'

CHAPTER SIXTY-THREE

The hollow emptiness caused by the loss of Emily would never heal, but Eliza knew she had to continue to live, and she learned to manage her grief.

Realising that Freddy had been pressured into acting so badly reassured her. He was a fool and he was weak, but he wouldn't let her down again. He'd bared his soul once he'd grasped the truth. Sam, clever Sam, had manipulated him shamefully.

'He wanted the old school building. He had a dream of building a shopping emporium there, of course, once we knew that couldn't happen he simply didn't know what to do. He'd met you and I think he saw a weakness. He always had a thing about…'

'…the Morgans? Yes, I know. I rather thought he'd have outgrown that nonsense. His complicated plotting ruined everything. If he'd been honest I'd have encouraged his plan, because it sounds like a good one, and I have no idea what to do with it. But that's Sam isn't it? He can't do the decent thing.'

CHAPTER SIXTY-FOUR

'I'm going to marry Sam and you can't stop me.'
Georgie spoke firmly, showing no sign of the simpering
child she'd been.

'He killed our beautiful Emily, he's a liar and
cheat, he tried to steal what was ours and has behaved in
the most dishonourable way. If you think you have fallen
in love with that, what could I possibly say to stop you?'

'Emily is dead because of me, and I'll never
forgive myself, but in my heart, I accept that we lost her
years ago. It's wicked and unjust, but it's the truth. I
refuse to fade away into the background for shame.

'I'll carry on living in the best way I can. I don't
want love, or romance. I want things, power, influence.

'But you'll never be able to trust him, you must
see that.'

'He's a lawyer, he's clever and determined. He's
the oldest son so one day he'll have the house and Aunt
Ellie's business. In the meantime, he has a great many
plans and I have every faith in him being able to provide
the life I want. I think we shall do very well together.'

'You appear to share his values, so yes, I imagine
you will.'

'Don't sneer, at least I know what I want.'

'You always know what you want, but it changes
from time to time. Once you wanted nothing more than
to be a Daventor.'

Georgie tutted. 'Yes, I once did. They've always
been fascinating to me. Their lives, their home, the
respect that they get wherever they go because of their

name, I wanted that, all of it. But then I realised how weak Freddy is. I don't want a weak man, I want someone with a bit of push, a man with the ability to get me what I want.'

Eliza felt sad, for herself and her silly, brittle sister.

'Do stop looking at me that way, as though I'm a puppy that just bit you.' Georgie snapped. 'Everything happened under your nose, not behind your back.'

'No more fighting, please Georgie. I'll wish you well in whatever you want to do, I promise.'

CHAPTER SIXTY-FIVE

Freddy followed Eliza through the gates of Sansome Springs, she'd decided exactly where she wanted to be standing when she told him her plans.

'I had an idea, just before Emily died, but when that happened I forgot everything for a while. I can't get the idea out of my mind now though, it's so clear and sharp. I can see it. I'll need a lot of help if I'm to see it to fruition, but I'd like to hear your opinion.'

Eliza took the rolled-up paper from under her arm. 'Here, help me straighten this out.'

She waited as he scrabbled for some smooth stones to hold the curling paper flat then watched as he studied the drawings, first from one side and then the other.

At last he looked up at her as the light began to dawn. 'Houses?'

Eliza nodded. 'Houses, with gardens, trees, room for vegetables, chickens, whatever. Stables and a road here. And then see, over here a row of shops.'

His eyes sparkled. 'Where is all of this?'

'It's what I'm going to build here.'

He drew in his breath sharply. 'You're building on sacred ground! Pass me your salts!' He slumped to the ground in a mock swoon, fanning his face with his hands.

'I know, I know. But seriously, what do you think?'

'Well, it is miserably shabby out here, if not downright dangerous.' He looked around slowly. 'If you don't do something it'll be wild again in a few years, nature is already trying to reclaim it.'

'That's what I've felt ever since we had our picnic there. But I didn't feel inclined to take on the worry, so I decided to sell it, then that dreadful actress of Sam's popped up. Then Emily and... well, I forgot everything.

'I can do anything I want with it. I don't have to keep it limping on as it is. I can build something truly lasting here.'

'And of course, you know so much about building houses.'

She put her hands on her hips. 'No. But you can introduce me to people that do.'

'Or you could just sell it all and let someone else have the headache.'

She shook her head. 'I overheard Uncle Hugh talking to a friend once at dinner. He'd inherited a patch of land he had no use for. He said he wanted to sell it. Hugh said you should never sell land. It will always pay you back in the end.

I knew I had to find the right thing for me to work with.'

She showed him the actual site that the first house would be built on.

'I find the thought exciting, whereas the very idea of learning how to manage a pleasure gardens filled me with dread.'

'Well, it's yours free and clear so I say, do what's going to make you happy. And it's not as though you've done anything in a rush.'

'I wanted to keep everything going along as it always had. But, things change, whether we want them to or not. Ruby wouldn't expect me to live off what she built, she'd encourage me to turn it into something relevant to me today.

'When that old woman gave her the land she didn't tell her what she could or couldn't do with it, it was hers to make of it what she could. Now it's mine.'

'The gardens will be altered beyond recognition, are you certain about this?'

'I've thought of nothing else for the past year. When these houses are built and occupied, I'm going to do the same thing again, three more times, one at each corner of the land. Four villages built around the spring.'

She saw the concern on his face and hastened to set his mind at ease. 'It will take years, but I'm in no hurry. I see this as my way of planting something new in Ruby's garden.'

'And this will all be gone?'

She nodded. 'The days of Sansome Springs are over.'

If you enjoyed this story you may also want to explore these titles from the same author:

The Harlot's Garden
The Harlot's Pride
The Harlot's Horde
Losing Hope
An Ordinary Girl

38678984R00145

Printed in Poland
by Amazon Fulfillment
Poland Sp. z o.o., Wrocław